Gringo

GRINGO

Terrell L. Bowers

AVALON BOOKS
THOMAS BOUREGY AND COMPANY, INC.
401 LAFAYETTE STREET
NEW YORK, NEW YORK 10003

© Copyright 1987 by Terrell L. Bowers
Library of Congress Catalog Card Number: 87-91568
ISBN 0-8034-8640-5

183 p.   בנאץ

PRINTED IN THE UNITED STATES OF AMERICA
BY HADDON CRAFTSMEN, SCRANTON, PENNSYLVANIA

Gringo

CHAPTER ONE

The judge looked over the papers in front of him, then scowled at Daniel Keen. It was easy for Dan to see that he'd reached the end of his rope this time. Judge Larsen had warned him twice before. This would certainly be Dan's last day with a badge.

"You seem to think that you're above our judicial system, Mr. Keen," Larsen said.

"No, sir," Dan replied quietly.

"Sixteen arrests this year, and you've killed seven men! What have you got to say about that?"

"If you'll check the records, your honor, you'll see that I've only been sent after the most dangerous men in the territory. No one else wanted to go after the guys I've tracked down."

"Now you're belittling the entire law in California! Maybe you'd like to sit up here and be the judge. Well, I don't try to act like God Himself, Deputy Keen. What

1

gives you the authority to be just that?"

"Cal Stelson was not going to give himself up to be hanged, your honor. He fired at me twice before I killed him. You've heard the witnesses back me up on that. I wasn't about to let the man empty his gun before I took him."

"And you gave me similar excuses for the other men you've killed, except for that renegade, Welch. You hardly tried to take him alive."

"He butchered a woman and her two children, your honor."

"There was no proof!"

"He had too many friends for that. But I still believe the dying breath of that woman, not the lying bunch of coyotes that man ran with. He'd have gotten away with murder!"

"That's precisely the attitude I've been talking about, Deputy Keen. You seem to think that you've been given some divine power to deal out justice on your own terms. In three years, you've been responsible for the death of twelve men."

"But what about all the arrests I've made? All but two of those men were hanged. If you send a badge after a hardened killer, the odds of taking him alive are slim, and you know it. He has nothing to lose by fighting to the death."

"I don't agree with you or your methods, Keen. As of this date, I'm removing you from the position of deputy U.S. marshal. Turn in your badge and pick up your things at the office. I don't expect to see you before me as an officer of the law again. If you ever set foot in my court as a defendant, I'll prosecute you to the fullest extent of the law."

"You're a real champion of justice, Judge Larsen," Dan said cynically. "You'd feel a mite different if any of the victims had been from your family. You can't be soft with vicious killers. It only makes them kill and plunder again. Don't you understand that, Judge?"

"I sincerely thank you for the lesson in social behavior, Mr. Keen. Now get out of my courtroom!"

Dan Keen pulled the badge from his shirt and tossed it to the floor. Then he turned and walked out of the courthouse, his heels pounding on the wooden boards with the force of his anger.

Once outside, he strode up the street to

the saloon. He wasn't much of a drinking man, but he needed something to quell his rancor. Sitting alone in a dark corner, he brooded over the quirks of fate that made him out to be the villain in a system that often allowed killers to run free.

The beer wasn't cold enough to be refreshing, so Dan sipped it and put it down on the table. He stared at the bubbles that rose from the bottom of the glass to the top. He studied the golden color and wondered what made beer smell stale.

The saloon was nearly empty so early in the day. Two businessmen were sitting across the room, and an early gambler was playing a hand of solitaire. The only other person there was the bartender.

Suddenly a young Mexican woman entered. Dan looked up at her with open curiosity, for she was not the sort of woman to frequent bars. She wore a crisp cotton riding skirt, and her hair was piled neatly on her head, held in place by a dark comb. She paused to let her eyes adjust to the gloomy interior of the saloon and then stared right at Dan.

He rose uncertainly to his feet as she approached his table.

"Might I speak with you, Mr. Keen?"

"By all means, little lady. Would you prefer to go someplace else?"

"Yes. I don't think a saloon is a proper place for a lady."

"I agree. Would you care for some lemonade? The cafe is just up the street."

"That would be more suitable."

He led the way out of the bar, holding the batwing door until the woman had passed through. As they headed for the cafe, Dan enjoyed the scent of her perfume and the whisper of her skirt. He had no idea who she was, but she was not a resident of the town. He'd surely have remembered such a lovely creature.

The girl didn't offer to speak until she was served a glass of lemonade. She took a dainty sip, then put her glowing eyes on Dan once more.

"My name is Juanita Mestas. My father owns a large rancho over at El Hueco. Have you heard of that place?"

"Near the California border, isn't it?"

"That's right. It has good grazing for horses and cattle."

"And which do you have?" Dan asked.

"Mostly cattle, except for our remuda.

We probably have forty head of horses."

"So what brings you here?"

"I'm looking for man...a man like you."

Dan blinked, then grinned. "This is a little sudden for me, ma'am. Besides which I always figured to do the asking for a woman's hand—not the other way around."

A spark of anger leapt into her eyes. "I don't have time for any silly jokes. I'm not in the habit of hiring men, but that's all I offer!"

"What makes you think I'm for hire?"

"You just lost your job as a lawman. You must want to face the future with some kind of work."

"So you know something about me already," he said.

"Daniel Keen, twenty-six years old, born in Vermont. But you came West at an early age. You served in the war and were promoted to captain of the California Volunteers. After the Civil War ended, you hired on as a town lawman. Then you became a United States deputy marshal. In three years, you've made fifty-one arrests and got convictions on all but two. And I think the judge went over your history of the past year."

"You've sure been checking up on me, Senorita. Now mind telling me why?"

"I need someone who is good with a gun, who is on the side of justice, who isn't afraid to kill."

"You want a hired gun, not an ex-lawman. I don't fancy hired killers. I've spent the last few years tracking down such vermin. I'd say you've come to the wrong man."

"I told you I wanted someone with a sense of justice. I'm not just hiring a gunman."

"Could have fooled me," Dan said.

"Are you interested or not?"

"You'll have to do a great deal more explaining about this whole thing. You may have a pretty face, but I won't die for it."

"You gringos are all alike! I thought that I could talk to you as a person. But you are just like all lowlife gringos!"

"You've got a winning way of presenting your arguments, Senorita, but the flattery won't work all by itself. You want to hire me. I want to know why."

The girl took a big swig of lemonade, as if the cool liquid would help to slake the angry fire in her veins. Then she looked at him again.

"A man called Roberto Martinez has been grabbing our land and our water. We have first access to the Rio Vagar. One very dry summer we sort of shared the water with him. He took advantage of the situation. He didn't go away.

"And now this man, Martinez, has hired killers to work for him. He has driven away many of our vaqueros, stolen cattle, and killed our livestock. I've lost two brothers and my mother to night raiders who attacked us and shot into our house."

"Sounds like a job for the law."

"What law?" she snapped. "You gringos have law only for yourselves. When a Mexican life is lost, you laugh about it. I know what you're like."

"If that's the way you feel, why come to me? Hire yourselves some gunmen of your own."

"Martinez has hired gringos. If we killed them, we'd bring the law down on ourselves." Juanita laughed bitterly. "It's all right for a gringo to kill a Mexican, but not for a Mexican to kill one of your kind!"

"That isn't always so, Senorita. One of the men I brought in last year had killed two Mexicans. He was hanged."

"That was here in Stockdale where a man like Judge Larsen presides. It's different at El Hueco where Abel Corman is the law. He can be paid to look the wrong way during a murder. So we have no hope for justice unless we hire a gringo lawman."

"As you said before, I'm no longer a lawman. I have no authority in El Hueco or any other place."

"You have your name and reputation. You're not afraid to fight other gringos." She let a cruel smile play on her lips. "And we'll pay you well. I've yet to see a gringo who doesn't have his price."

Dan shook his head while leaving enough coins on the table to cover the price of their lemonades. He slid back his chair and stood up.

"You have such a wholesome, open-minded attitude about Americans, about men like me. Maybe you'll have better luck with the next gringo you try to hire. I told you before, I don't kill for money. I've only killed men in the line of duty. They were

all killers themselves. I've never shot anyone who wasn't trying to shoot me as well.
So you can take your offer and your beautiful self right back to El Hueco. I'm not your
man."

With that he left the cafe. He didn't even
know where he was going. But he had to
get away, get out of town, get off alone
where a man could think.

CHAPTER TWO

The spot Dan had picked was not the best place to fish—he'd had no bites so far. But it was green, it was cool, and it was quiet. Fishing was good for steadying a man's nerves. It wasn't important that he really catch anything.

As Dan leaned against a crooked oak tree, he thought about the men who had died under his gun. He was not cold-blooded. He'd never shot a man needlessly, never put an extra bullet into a downed gunman. He knew in his heart that he'd told the judge the truth. He'd killed twelve criminals over the years because he always drew the toughest assignments. He hadn't enjoyed the shootings. He'd merely taken his role seriously, doing a dirty job that had to be done. Some men got into farming, storekeeping, drumming, or whatever, and Dan Keen had gotten into law enforcement.

The sound of an approaching rider broke into his thoughts. He glanced over his shoulder to see the Mexican girl again. She was heading toward him, wearing a hat this time. It was tipped to the side of her head, her hair down now and loose about her shoulders.

"Let me guess," he said dryly as she dismounted and hitched her horse to a shrub. "You want to know if these fish only bite on gringo bait, or if Mexicans can also catch them."

"You make fun of my predicament."

"I didn't mean to. You're welcome to drown a worm wherever you please."

"I didn't come here to fish," Juanita said.

"That can only mean trouble for me. What's on your mind this time?"

"Maybe I misjudged you, Mr. Keen. Could we discuss a working arrangement?"

"No, I don't think so. On top of everything else, you don't like gringos, and I wouldn't like working for a woman. It isn't anything against you personally. I'm just not the type of man to take orders from a female."

"Why should it matter who you work for?

Doesn't a job and good pay mean anything to you?"

"Not the kind of job you have in mind. I don't intend to end up killing someone in a range war."

"You were a lawman for several years! Can't you see our situation as one that needs such a form of justice? Don't we deserve a chance to live in peace?"

"If you want a gunman, hire someone else."

"I'm desperate, Mr. Keen. I don't know where else to turn." She sat down next to him.

"There are lots of men in any town who'd fight for you."

"Not against Colin Wyatt and his two guns."

Dan's head snapped around. "Colin Wyatt! You're bucking a man like Colin Wyatt?"

"I told you that you were the one for this job. Who else would go up against someone like him?"

"I'm flattered you think me so capable, ma'am. But I'm not in the same class with him. Why, he's killed thirty men or more, and he's as pleasant as a stepped-on rattle-snake!"

"Mr. Keen, I...I'm not very good at asking for something. Especially from a grin—an American."

"You needn't worry," Dan said. "Of all the people in the world, Americans are the least offended by slang names. Must be the brass we have."

"As I was saying, I'm not good at crawling before some high-handed, arrogant gringo!" Juanita snapped.

"Quit buttering me up and say what's on your mind."

"They'll hang my brother!" she blurted out in frustration. "They've already sentenced him. He only has three days left to live unless you'll help me!"

"I thought your brothers were killed by raiders," Dan said.

"Two of them were killed. Pepe is the only brother I have left, and he's going to hang in three days. I must get help to stop them from killing him!"

"If he's been legally sentenced to hang, I don't see where I'd be of any help," Dan said. "I'm not the kind to break someone out of jail and get my own face pasted on a wanted poster."

"But he's innocent!"

"Never met a man about to be hanged that wasn't. Can't expect a sane man to admit to a hanging offense."

Juanita glared at him for a long moment. "You are a worthless man!" she finally exploded. "Can't you see that only someone like you can save my brother from death? We're willing to pay you whatever you ask. Well, what we can afford, anyway. We were once a very rich family. My father will make you a well-rewarded man."

"A well-rewarded corpse would be more like it," Dan said. "Colin Wyatt plays for keeps. Drawing against him and his two guns would be throwing away my life— even if I was on the right side of the law."

The girl furiously kicked the ground, knocking loose dirt and dried leaves into Dan's face. Then she unhitched her horse and mounted it, exposing a shapely bit of leg.

"I hope you enjoy sitting here and wasting your life, Mr. Keen. In fact, I hope you become part of the earth, rotting away to the moldering bag of bones that you are made of!"

Dan smiled broadly. "Thank you, ma'am. Always a pleasure having words with a charming lady like yourself."

Juanita jerked the reins of her horse, uttering something under her breath that could have been a Mexican profanity. Then she put her heels to the mount and tore off at a full gallop.

Watching her disappear, Dan stopped smiling. He wondered if her brother had been framed, if she was truly desperate for help. She'd sounded desperate enough.

Fishing had lost its appeal for Dan. He would find no peace of mind now sitting under the shade tree, thinking about his future. All the same, he had to make plans. He'd heard that the Texas Rangers were hiring able men. Maybe he should go there and see for himself.

"No time like the present to get started," he said aloud, pulling in his fishing line. Juanita had ruined his afternoon, so he might as well get a good meal and a good night's rest, then put his job, the judge, and the town of Stockdale behind him.

* * *

The three riders on the trail ahead of Dan were only shadows among the tall trees. He had no trouble identifying the one on the big sorrel as the senorita. It appeared that she was so desperate that she was trying to hire any gringos she ran into. At least that was what Dan thought at first.

But then she suddenly struck out at one rider with her quirt and bucked her horse between the two men. Dan jerked his own horse to a stop, startled at her abrupt move. To his surprise, Juanita raced to him, sliding her horse to a jolting stop in front of him.

"Please, Mr. Keen!" she gasped. "Please help me!"

The two men came after her, but they slowed at once, seeing that something new had been added to the picture—Dan Keen.

Not knowing what was going on, Dan automatically cocked his gun, keeping his hand on the butt, watching the two hard cases approach. From experience, he knew what kind of men he was up against. He'd have bet his saddle and tack that the pair had their faces on wanted posters.

Juanita swung her horse about, boldly

facing the two riders. "They're killers for
Martinez," she said under her breath.
"They want to keep me from hiring any
help."

Both men stopped at a distance of twenty
feet, dirty, narrow-eyed, suspicious. Like
Dan, they had their hands on their guns.

"What's the problem here?" Dan asked,
making his voice pleasant.

"No problem, mister," one of the two
said. "This here is a runaway from El
Hueco. Her pa hired us to fetch her back.
She ain't of legal age yet."

"That's right," the other man joined in.
"This little wildcat can spout lies quicker
than most men can think. She's conned a
number of men already. Hope you didn't
fall for none of her tales."

Dan flicked a glance at the girl. "That
right, ma'am? You been telling me
stories?"

"No!" she cried. "They work for Martinez! They want to take me back to El
Hueco!"

"Don't recollect anyone named Martinez," the first man said thoughtfully. "We
were hired by her father, Hernando

Mestas. He's worried to death about his little girl."

"They're lying!" Juanita fired back. "You must help me, Dan Keen!"

The two men exchanged glances. No doubt they had heard of the ex-U.S. deputy marshal.

"I don't suppose her father wrote you up some kind of order or permission to take his runaway daughter home?" Dan said.

The second one shrugged. "You know how it is. We didn't think she'd ever get so far away."

"Wyatt didn't think she'd actually get help, did he?" Dan asked.

The first one opened his mouth to answer before he realized that Dan had set him up. Then both men began to draw their guns.

Dan's reaction was too quick for them. He had them both covered before they could shoot.

"Let's not do anything hasty, boys," Dan said in his cold, authoritative voice. "I'd hate to kill a couple of men for no reason."

Both men slowly raised their hands.

The first one glared openly at the girl. "I don't know what lies this spitfire has fed you, mister, but you've got us dead wrong. We were hired to come bring her back to her father."

"I'll admit spitfire is the right name for her," Dan said. "But I'm not so sure that it was her father who hired you. Why don't you carefully drop your guns and rifles?"

The second rider said, "You're making a mistake, Keen. This ain't none of your affair!"

"Just do as I say. I don't want any killing over this."

The men obeyed, dropping their guns and belts into the dirt at the feet of the horses. When Dan told them to ride off, they didn't stick around and argue. They just headed toward town.

"Now do you believe me?" Juanita asked.

"I'll say one thing for you, woman. You have the good sense to stay out of the fight. On the other hand, you suckered me into a move that might have gotten me killed."

"Are you such a coward? Have you no courage, no honor?"

He shook his head, stepping down from his horse to gather up the guns. "The secret of a long life, Senorita, is not to do dumb things that might shorten it. I don't want to be mixed up in your private war. As I've already told you, I'm not a gun for hire."

Her black eyes flashed. "You stood up to those two gringos! You were willing to fight them! Why can't you help save my brother?"

"It's not up to me. I'm no longer carrying a badge. You need to get the U.S. marshal to intervene. Even an order from Judge Larsen might help. He's got pull. Hiring a gunman to match Colin Wyatt is no easy chore, and it'll only build up your war with Martinez. Guns and killing are not the answer."

As he remounted his horse, Juanita threw a string of Spanish words in his direction, all of them less than flattering. Then she left him behind, charging off toward Stockdale.

Dan sighed deeply. "Why do I get the feeling that I'm not really making points with that gal?" he said aloud.

Then he was also heading for town. But he rode very, very slowly. He wanted to do some thinking.

CHAPTER THREE

"But I'm an American citizen!" Juanita said. "I was born in California! I went to American schools. I have rights like all other Americans!"

"I sympathize with you, Miss Mestas," Judge Larsen said quietly. "But I have no authority to look into the matter in El Hueco. You would have to file an appeal with a higher court to get an injunction to stop the hanging of your brother. Unless things somehow come to Stockdale, there is nothing I can do."

"But how do I get such an order?"

"You would have to go to Los Angeles and present your case. If things are the way you describe, I think you'd get a postponement."

"There isn't time! They'll hang my brother in three days!"

The judge lowered his head sorrowfully.

"I'm very sorry, miss, but I have no power to stop such things."

Tears burned Juanita's eyes, but she blinked them away irritably. She had hoped against all odds, ridden off against her father's wishes, faced the open country alone, risked her life against men like Bobby Leets and Clay Yorker, the two who'd been driven off by Dan Keen. All of those things had not stopped her. It was the law itself that was her most potent enemy. That and time.

She left the judge's chambers and went to the cafe. Sitting at the very table where she and Dan had talked, Juanita ordered a light supper. She was not the least bit hungry, but she knew she must keep up her strength. She couldn't give up. Somehow she had to save Pepe. In three days' time he would hang. She had to find a way to prevent that.

Even as Juanita sat dejectedly alone, she glimpsed Dan Keen riding into town. He made his way to the small building that had the word JAIL painted above the door. With an armload of guns, he went into the small office. At least he had done that much for her. Without the ex-lawman, she'd have been forced to return to El Hueco with the two men. She had no desire to be around such scum.

"Would you like anything more?" asked the woman running the cafe.

Yes, she thought to herself. I'd like Dan Keen on my side. Instead of speaking, however, she only shook her head negatively.

As Juanita ate, she kept thinking about Pepe. She had no sisters. And he was the only brother she had left. He was two years younger than her own nineteen, much too young to die at the end of a rope. Especially for a crime he didn't commit!

Dan took a last look at his cards and tried to hide his disappointment. He was down ten dollars, but he was smart enough to know that was as close to even as he was likely to get. He was not a real gambler. He played occasionally for relaxation, for the fun of the game, not to earn money. Long nights of sitting at smoke-filled tables and risking everything on a few cards was not the thing for him.

"I think I'll call it a night," he said when the hand was played. "You boys can look around for a different sucker—one with more money than me—to sit in."

Two of the four remaining men laughed as Dan left the saloon, going out into the night air.

Always cautious, he kept to the shadows. He had crossed two men earlier that day. He didn't intend to give them a chance to get back at him. His walk to the hotel was uneventful, with no suspicious men lurking in doorways or alleys. He decided there was a good chance the two gunmen were not really concerned about him. Maybe they had already returned to El Hueco or were busy planning another method for getting the girl back to her hometown.

A pang of guilt went through Dan. Those two gunmen added substance to the girl's story. He could easily picture Colin Wyatt ordering them to bring Juanita back to El Hueco.

All the same, if her brother had been legally tried and sentenced to hang, there wasn't a blessed thing he could do to prevent it. He surely wouldn't break her brother out of jail. What did she expect him to do?

Dan's thoughts had kept him preoccupied on the way to his room. He stopped at once now, for he could see the glimmer of light under his door. He was certain that he hadn't been the one who had lighted the lamp!

Carefully, his gun already in his right hand, he turned the doorknob with his left. When he pushed the door open, he was ready to blast away.

Juanita sucked in her breath, shocked that he had entered the room ready to shoot.

"What are you doing here?" he asked, closing the door and holstering his gun. "I might have killed you."

"I—I was..." She cleared her throat, got up from her chair, and walked toward him. "I wanted to thank you, Mr. Keen," she said. "You saved my life today."

He frowned, searching her face, wondering what to expect next. To his utter astonishment, Juanita put her arms around him and kissed him. It was quite an overwhelming experience.

"I want you to save my brother," she whispered softly. "If you will just—"

"You little vixen!" Dan snapped, pushing her away. "I never thought you'd try anything this dumb, this cheap! Now get out of my room!"

He was ready for the swing she took at him, catching her wrist in his hand. Then, without realizing he was going to do it, he pulled her toward him for a rough, punishing kiss. This time it was Juanita who pushed him away.

"Don't like your own medicine, do you?" he said.

"I must have been crazy to think that I could appeal to your better nature. You make me sick!"

"Please leave. And pronto!"

Juanita marched past Dan and slammed the door behind her. He could almost smell the smoke from her fiery temper. She was one determined young woman. But his gun was not for sale.

Dan walked over to the window and looked down at the street. He grinned at the small-framed figure that walked out of the hotel. The girl was still fuming. Her angry footsteps told him that.

Two shadows suddenly appeared, one of them throwing a hand over the girl's mouth. Then Juanita was dragged quickly into the darkness.

"Not again," Dan groaned, already rushing out of his room.

He dashed down the stairs, certain Juanita was being abducted by the same two mangy coyotes he'd encountered earlier today. Not seeing anyone in the street, Dan darted toward the livery stable, a likely destination for the trio. He had not gone far before he heard the two men.

"Ow!" one of them cried. "Get hold of her feet!"

"You hold her feet!" the other one snarled. "She almost knocked my teeth out. Look, I'm bleeding!"

"Blast your hide, woman!" the first one said. "You quit fighting us, or I'll bust you a good one!"

Dan heard a smack, then joined the trio. Soon there was a mass of arms and legs as all four of them piled onto the ground.

Some unexpected rain poured down about the time Dan was planting a foot in one man's stomach and pulling a handful of the other's hair. With his free hand, he began to punch the second man's face. But just then the girl kicked him, knocking him over backward.

The two men tried to grab Juanita again,

but she was clawing and kicking, while cursing them in Spanish. Then Dan got into action, and the bruised gunmen escaped into the torrential downpour.

Juanita was panting for breath, her wet hair pasted down on her head, her clothes muddy and torn.

Dan sat there, his hand on his gun, looking out into the watery night. Then he put his eyes on Juanita and grinned.

"You surely do liven up a man's life, Juanita. Can't say that I've ever met a woman who caused more excitement than you."

"Why did you come after me?"

"I saw the two men grab you. I just happened to be looking out my window."

"Laughing at my shattered dignity, no doubt," she said.

Dan got to his feet and offered the girl a hand. She came up from the puddles uncertainly. He put an arm around her and made his way back to the hotel porch. He released her there.

"As much as I hate to admit it, I'm in debt a second time, Dan Keen," she said.

"You're quite a woman, Juanita. A good many men would die for a chance to simply put their arms around you."

"But not you," she said. "You wouldn't help me when I kissed you and begged you to save my brother's life." Her voice was soft, but her fury boiled just beneath the surface.

"You shouldn't have done that."

Juanita's face was suffused with embarrassment. It made her more beautiful— even standing there dripping wet, covered with mud.

"I . . . I apologize for that. I'm not used to lowering myself to such things."

"Such things as kissing a gringo?"

The fire instantly leapt back into her eyes. "As kissing anyone! I was desperate for help! I would do almost anything to save my brother's life!"

"You'd even go so low as to kiss me."

"Exactly!" she snapped, splashing across the street toward a boardinghouse.

She slipped, cursed the mud, and stomped onward. The only thing Dan could do was smile and shake his head.

CHAPTER FOUR

Juanita didn't try to hide her surprise at finding Dan at the livery stable, his horse saddled and waiting. She ordered a hostler to fetch her own sorrel before she even attempted to speak to Dan.

"I don't understand, Mr. Keen. From the way you acted, what you said, I—"

"Don't read too much into my being here, ma'am," he cautioned her. "I'll ride down to El Hueco and see what's going on. I can't promise that I'll be able to help."

"Bobby and Clay may try and stop you," Juanita said a few moments later, mounting her horse.

"Those the two fellers we've been having run-ins with?"

"Bobby Leets and Clay Yorker. They're the scum of the earth, two-bit killers, but not when facing anyone. It's your back you have to worry about with such men. But I still don't understand your coming to El

31

Hueco. Why the change of heart?"

Dan smiled. "Maybe that kiss worked after all. I haven't been able to get you out of my head."

"Before we leave, just how much money are you demanding for your services?"

"I'll have to wait and see what help I can be. If there's nothing I can do, then there's no deal."

"I must tell you here and now, there will be no more kissing between us. Not ever. Understand?'

"Sure. After all, I'm only a gringo with a gun. I'd have no right to think of any romantic links between us."

"That's right," she said firmly. "I wanted to make that very clear."

The rest of the morning passed in total silence. It was only when they stopped to eat that Juanita spoke again.

"The valley on the other side of the mountain gap was settled by my family before the fighting over Texas. We have lived there for many years now. Of course more families have moved in, and the population has grown. There are now farmers in the valley, and the land is spread among many. We were doing fine until Roberto Martinez drove his herds of cattle onto the free range opposite our valley. He's like a great funnel, sucking in land, water, and power. The men he hired were tough and troublesome. Many of the farmers were chased off the land they'd owned for years. The man's greed knows no bounds. He means to own the entire valley, push everyone else out, before he's finished."

"How many gunmen does he have?" Dan asked.

"There are a hundred vaqueros working for him, but only a handful of hired gunmen. Colin Wyatt has four main hard cases: Bobby and Clay—who you've met—and Pancho Valdez and Rico Lucinda. The five of them have caused most of the deaths in our town."

"What about you? Who's on your side?" Dan asked.

"The entire valley looks to us to stop the bloodshed, to somehow put an end to the tyranny. But we've got no fighters working for us now. My two older brothers were fighters. It cost them their lives."

"No one else?"

"We're down to a skeleton crew of about fifteen men or so. What can we do against such odds? My father is nearly sixty years old and not in good health. The sheriff is Martinez's pawn. It's shameful. He doesn't investigate ranch killings or raids. He says he's only concerned with what happens in town."

"Jurisdiction limitation, huh?" Dan said.

Juanita nodded solemnly.

"How'd your brother end up in jail awaiting a rope?"

"They say he killed Jake Blair, a farmer, by shooting him, but that man was a friend of ours," Juanita said.

"Any witnesses?"

"Pancho Valdez and Bobby Leets. They said they saw Pepe leaving Jake's farm just before the fire broke out that ruined his farm. According to Valdez and Leets, they were being good neighbors, racing over to fight the fire. But it was too late to save Jake."

"What was their reason for being at the scene of the crime?" Dan asked.

"They work for Martinez. They don't need any reasons."

"Who presided at the trial?"

"Judge Dick Haller. He's bought and

paid for, no more than a second pawn for Martinez. The jury was picked from town. And they were all afraid of Martinez. To cross him would mean death to themselves or their families."

"What on earth makes you think that bringing me into El Hueco will be of any help? You don't need one man. You need a small army."

"What am I supposed to do?" Juanita asked. "I had to get some kind of help. My brother will die the day after tomorrow!"

Dan let out a long, deep breath. "All I'm trying to say, Senorita, is there's not much I can do. Without authority of some kind, we have no way to postpone that hanging."

"But you're a well-known lawman. People will listen to you," Juanita said.

"I no longer carry a badge. Or have you forgotten that little detail?"

"They won't have to know that."

"You forget your two pals, Clay and Bobby," Dan said. "It's likely they learned of my dismissal in Stockdale. It's tough to pretend you have a flush with only three cards."

"I don't know how to gamble, but I understand what you're saying."

"Then my trip is a waste of time for both of us."

"So leave!" she snapped. "Turn your back like the other gringos. Pretend that we Mexicans aren't human!"

"You do have a short fuse, spitfire," Dan said.

"Don't call me that!"

"What would you prefer—hellcat?"

"My name is Juanita Mestas! You can call me Senorita Mestas or Miss Mestas."

"Too formal," he grunted.

"I insist on a certain amount of dignity."

"Way I see it, you've got no call to insist on anything. After all, you came to my hotel room, you kissed me, you asked for my help."

"I knew you would throw that silly business in my face! How typical of a lowly, indolent gringo!"

Dan's eyes flicked past the girl. He'd thought the brush had moved but hadn't been certain until that moment.

"Admit it, spitfire. You're interested in me. That's what really sticks in your craw, isn't it? You'd like to hate my guts, but you're really sort of falling in love with me."

"What?" The girl was incredulous. "Why, you arrogant, self-centered, conceited—"

Dan drew his gun and fired, all in one motion. And Juanita cried out in alarm. But before her scream died away, Clay Yorker fell into the clearing.

Not waiting for Bobby to find a target, Dan rolled into a clump of brush. He didn't figure any man would dare shoot a woman like Juanita, regardless of the situation. The sound of a horse's retreating hoofbeats told him he'd guessed right. He stood up, gun still cocked and ready, and could see the rider and horse race away at breakneck speed.

"You called that shot, ma'am," he told a very shaky Juanita. "Only getting you riled kept Clay from blasting me. I think he was enjoying the tongue-lashing I was getting."

Juanita was still trembling. She looked at the body of Clay Yorker, then turned to Dan. Her lips parted, but no words came out.

"I don't know if we should take the body

into El Hueco," Dan said. "There might be some accusations against me."

"W-what choice do we have?" Juanita finally said in a trembling voice.

"I'll take him back to Stockdale and tell Larsen what happened, though he might just lock me up until there's a hearing."

"You can't go back! What about my brother?"

Dan shook his head sadly. "I don't see any way to save him, ma'am. I really don't."

"But there has to be a way!"

"Not legally, and I imagine Martinez will see that there are lots of guards to keep the boy in jail until he walks to the rope. I'm afraid I can't help you."

"He's only a boy," she cried, tears shining brightly in her eyes.

"I'll have to ask you for a deposition, a statement about how Clay was getting set to kill me. Then I'll take his body back to Stockdale."

"And there is nothing you can do to save my brother from death?"

"I'm really sorry, Miss Mestas, but the law's hands are tied. There just isn't time

to get a stay of execution or postponement."

The girl was stricken with grief, but she
still managed to write down a statement
for Dan to show Judge Larsen.

Dan helped her get on her horse and put
her on the road to El Hueco. He could see
her shoulders slumped in defeat, but there
was nothing he could do.

CHAPTER FIVE

Standing under the warm afternoon sun, Juanita did not watch the train pull out. She was looking into the distance, seeing nothing. As the caboose passed behind the stoutly built jail, she continued to stare off into the great beyond. How could she confront her brother now?

Sighing deeply, she walked over to the building. The guard met her at the door, with a second and third man—Martinez men—visible inside. They were taking no chances on a break.

"What do you want, Juanita?" Sheriff Corman asked her outright.

"I'd like to visit my brother."

"Five minutes is all you get, and no tricks. You try and pass him a gun, you'll be right in there with him."

"I'm not such a fool," she told him flatly. "May I see him now?"

The sheriff stepped aside to allow her to

walk into the office. She hated the way
Colin Wyatt leered at her. She felt dirty,
just having his eyes roam over her. Rico
was not any better, laughing as if he'd just
heard a vulgar joke. Juanita did her best to
ignore the two of them, going through the
office door to the cell in back.

Pepe was on his feet, his young, anxious
face pressed against the bars. He was pale
with worry and apprehension, his eyes
showing a redness from uncharacteristic
crying. His courage had run dry. Looking
at his sister, he could read the regret and
anguish in her features. She didn't have to
tell him that she'd failed.

"Good to see you, Juanita." He forced a
bit of bravado into his voice for her sake.
"Guess you didn't have any luck?"

"There just wasn't time," she said huskily. "I thought I'd found a man to help, but
Clay and Bobby tried to ambush us. He
killed Clay and took him back to Stockdale. He seemed to think the situation was
hopeless."

"It is," Pepe said quietly.

"I'm so ... so ..."

Pepe held up his hand to silence her.
"You did what you could, Juanita. I can

only hope you and Papa fare better against Martinez than I did at the trial."

"Papa wants to come in and take you away from Corman and the others."

Pepe said, "Why do you think Colin Wyatt is here? And Rico? They are waiting for Papa to do something foolish, so they can kill him legally—just like me."

"He's a desperate man, Pepe. You're his last remaining son, the only one to carry on his name. He feels he has to do something."

"All the same, Juanita, you keep him out of town for the big event. I don't want to have any of you see me hanged. Come take me home when it's..." His voice broke. He could not finish.

"If it's your last wish, I'll try and keep Papa and the others at home."

Pepe bobbed his head, no longer trusting his voice to speak without cracking. He put a hand through the bars to Juanita. She took it between her own and held it to her cheek, dampening it with the tears she couldn't control.

"Time's up!" Abel Corman snapped. "Say your good-bys and be done with it, Senorita."

Juanita let go of Pepe, turning her hurt into anger. She stormed over to the sheriff. He regarded her coolly.

"How do you sleep at nights, you sniveling coward?" Juanita snapped. "You know Pepe didn't kill anyone!"

"Jury found differently," Colin Wyatt said.

"Your jury!" she fired at the gunman. "You filthy murderers killed Jake Blair! It was on your boss's orders that an innocent farmer was killed, just so you could accuse my brother of murder. You sit here and laugh about his hanging. He's only a boy. What vermin you are!"

"Senorita Mestas, you'll have to leave." The sheriff took her by the arm. He practically dragged her through the office and pushed her out into the street.

"You are as guilty as they are!" she shouted at Abel Corman. "You represent the law, but you defile justice and everything it stands for!"

"I didn't sentence the boy to hang, Juanita. If you want to hate someone, hate the members of the jury."

She might have cursed him longer, but he closed the door in her face. Filled with helpless frustration, she could only turn and start for home. She would respect her brother's last wish. She would keep her father from mounting an attack that would surely get all their ranch hands killed.

The midnight train would soon pull out. It had stopped only for water and for some packages that were being shipped out of El Hueco.

Dan secured the length of rope and went up to the nearest jail window. He pulled a trash can over, turned it upside down, and stood on it. From his perch he could look right into the small cell at the rear of the jail.

The Mexican youth was not sleeping away his last hours on earth. He had been kneeling at the bed, praying for some miracle to save his life.

"Ask and it shall come to you," Dan whispered.

The young man looked up in surprise. With a strange fascination he watched Dan tie the rope around the window bars.

"When the window goes, you climb out of there pronto," Dan instructed him. "Get to the rear of the train as fast as you can!"

The boy looked into the next room. The three men were sacked out on the floor, all sleeping with guns at their sides. He would have to move fast or be killed trying to escape. Still, it was more of a chance than he'd have against a rope. He nodded his understanding.

Dan moved into the darkness and waited for the train to pull out. He had his hand on his gun, but he didn't want to get into any fights. What he was doing could land him behind bars for a number of years. He didn't like that feeling one bit.

All at once the train lurched into motion. The rope's slack was taken up shortly. And when the barred window gave way, half of the wall collapsed!

Shouts came from within the building, but Pepe dashed out into the darkness. His legs were pumping after the train. He spotted Dan at the open boxcar and raced up to jump into the opening.

Dan pulled the boy aboard and urged the train to more speed. As luck would have it, the men in the jail were confused and unable to find their way through the cloud of dust and steam. When they appeared at the edge of the tracks, the train had al-

ready run a hundred yards and was picking up steam.

"That's just perfect." Dan grinned. "By
the time they get horses, we'll be in the
clear."

Pepe said, "But they'll catch the train.
The grade up ahead is very steep!"

"That's what I'm counting on, Pepe."

"Who are you? Why are you doing this
for me?"

"I'm not doing it for you exactly. Your
sister got me into this mess. It'll be up to
you to keep me from getting killed over
this."

"What can I do? I'm a condemned man!"

"No time for that now," Dan said. "Follow me."

He crossed to the opposite side of the
boxcar and looked out into the blackness.
The train was rolling at a good clip now,
getting up a full head of steam for the long
pull that lay just up the tracks another
mile.

Dan took hold of Pepe's arm, standing in
the door, looking into the dark. "When I
say jump, you come with me. I've got two
horses stashed out in the trees. By the time

Colin runs down the train, we'll be miles in the other direction."

"I still don't—" Pepe began.

"Jump!"

Dan didn't just call it out, he jerked the boy with him. They landed in a roll, going down the side of a hill in a tumble and slide. When they stopped at the bottom, Dan grabbed Pepe once more and took him quickly toward the waiting horses.

The escape was a good one. Dan and Pepe passed town shortly after Colin and his men rode out after the train. Dan figured they had at least a two-hour head start. With the horse he'd provided for Pepe, the boy could make it to Stockdale and safety.

"I don't understand this," Pepe said. "You want me to escape to Stockdale and give myself up to be hanged?"

"Judge Larsen will have you in custody, Pepe. He gave me his word that he would slow down extradition as long as possible. And if at all feasible, you'll have another trial there. First, though, I'll have some time to find out who really killed that farmer."

"Knowing that Colin Wyatt arranged to have it done won't make it any easier to prove. I don't see how this can keep my neck out of a noose."

"You'll have to do as I say, Pepe. It's the only chance you have to help yourself and your family. Believe me, I wouldn't risk going to prison for nothing."

"This Judge Larsen, he must be a friend of yours."

"Hardly that. Your sister spoke to him and won his sympathy. He thinks I'm a troublemaker with too quick a trigger finger."

"That makes me feel much better," Pepe grunted.

"Get going," Dan told him. "Just ride into Stockdale and turn yourself over to Larsen. I'll handle things at this end. Let's hope for another trial."

Pepe grinned. "Sure, what have I got to lose? I was going to hang later today. Let me tell you, a condemned man savors the hours like a fine meal. I'll be happy at least to have a few more meals before my time is up."

"With luck, maybe that time won't be up for another fifty years," Dan said.

"I hope you're right."

"Get going."

The young man took off into the blackness of night. Once he got to the main trail, he would have no trouble finding his way.

As for Dan Keen, he would spend a full day away from El Hueco to throw off any suspicion that he'd helped Pepe break out of jail. Then his real chore would start—proving Pepe's innocence.

CHAPTER SIX

Roberto Martinez was not the kind of man to take defeat lightly. He roared and he swore, pacing the floor like an enraged bear. He slammed his fist against the wall and kicked over a chair. His anger was not controllable. His passions were violent.

"I don't believe this!" he screamed at Colin Wyatt. "How could you let that little mouse escape?"

"He had help. I told you about the bars being tied to the train. Someone arranged the jailbreak and then had a horse waiting for him."

"And you've found no trace of Mestas?"

"He headed over to the main road. By the time we picked up his trail, a dozen animals had passed in that direction and a couple of wagons. There was a second horse, but it disappeared into the Rio Vagar. We couldn't find where it got back out."

"You couldn't find your hat with both hands—if it was still on your head!" Martinez roared.

Colin turned red, his own temper rising. But he suppressed it.

"The question is, what do you want us to do now?"

"The other horse probably belonged to that wildcat, Juanita. I think you should send Rico over to ask her about it. He has a way with the ladies, does he not?"

Colin shrugged. "He beat his wife to death with his fists, if that's what you mean. The man likes to hurt people."

"Precisely," Martinez said smugly. "I think he's just the man to speak to Juanita about that escape."

"What about Clay Yorker? We going to do anything about him being killed?"

"Yes," Martinez said. "Hire that pair of bounty hunters in town. I want enough guns to take care of whatever happens. They can be bought cheap."

"Want to put them to work on the ranch or do they just sit around town?"

"Give them some drinking money and let them stay in town. I want to know what's going on. If there's a lead on Pepe Mestas, we'll send them to collect him."

Colin left the room after taking some money from Martinez. When he exited the house, Bobby, Rico, and Pancho Valdez were waiting. He told Bobby and Pancho to get some rest. Then he explained what he wanted from Rico.

"I hear the boss man holler." Rico grinned, his thin lips curling at the corners. "He is like a tiger, that one."

Colin said, "Someday he'll shout one too many words at me. I'll take off my spurs and shove them down his throat!"

"But not until the money play out—is true?"

Colin chuckled, releasing some of his own pent-up emotions. "Go ask the senorita what she knows about her brother's escape. But don't rush into anything. Take your time. Wait around all day long if you have to. Only, get her when she's all alone. Don't let anyone see you. Understand?"

"Si." A look of pleasure crossed Rico's face.

Then the Mexican hurried off to find his horse. Colin didn't care for Rico's enthusiasm. He resented the high-and-mighty attitude of the senorita, but he wasn't fond of hurting women or children. Call him what they might, he'd never struck a woman, never harmed a child.

He wandered off after his own mount, thinking how Rico had once bragged about the way he handled *his* women. Rico was one of those lowlifes who thought might made right. Knocking some poor woman around made him feel bigger. In Colin's estimation, that made him all the smaller. But that was why Martinez had chosen Rico to talk to Juanita.

Dan Keen was a shadow, a wisp of dust that drifted on the wind and disappeared into thin air. He spent a full day riding around, looking over the lay of the land. By the time he crossed onto Mestas property, the sun was lowering on the horizon. He hoped to find a glen for himself and his horse and spend a peaceful night. But that was not to be.

The two men rode out of the trees, guns leveled, no warmth in their eyes. Dan stopped his horse and raised his hands carefully above his shoulders.

"Afternoon, boys," he said with an uncertain smile. "You work for Mestas?"

"Is a gringo," one man said to the other. "What do we do with him, Bernardo?"

"Juanita say to kill all gringos. They are working with Martinez."

"Not me," Dan said. "I came to see Juanita's father."

"He come to kill Hernando, Fernandez. We should shoot him and be done with it!"

"I'm telling you, I'm not working for Martinez. Juanita hired me over in Stockdale. I'm the man who killed Clay Yorker."

The two men exchanged looks.

Dan said, "Take me to Juanita. She'll tell you who I am."

"I think he lie, Fernandez," Bernardo said. "But you're the foreman."

"Juanita will wring your neck, Bernardo, if you kill me," Dan said. "I'm telling you the truth. You've probably seen her temper."

"Perhaps this man is who he claims," Fernandez said, lowering his gun slightly.

"Juanita is doing laundry at the river," Bernardo said. "We will take you to her. If you have lied to us, she will carve out your heart."

"Knowing her, I don't doubt that one bit, fellows."

The two men didn't grin or show any signs of thawing as they led Dan to the river.

Juanita struggled, but she could not keep from swallowing another mouthful of muddy water. Only when her lungs seemed about to burst did the man's rough hand jerk her head back up.

"Next time, I might not let you up at all, Senorita. You tell me what I want to know, or I'll drown you here and now!"

"B-but I don't know—"

Rico pushed Juanita's head back into the water.

Terror ripped at her heart, her panic swelling like a balloon. Rico was not going to let her up this time!

In desperation, Juanita tried to move farther into the river, pulling Rico a little deeper into the water. He only held on to her more tightly.

He's going to kill me! I'm going to die!
her mind screamed.

Somehow that thought helped her get
her head back above the water. But not for
long.

Rico pushed her down again with great
force.

Coming within view of the river, the two
Mexicans were temporarily too dumb-
founded to move. But Dan instantly
spurred his horse right at Juanita's assail-
ant, forcing him to let go of the girl.

As Bernardo and Fernandez pulled a
coughing and choking Juanita out of the
water, Dan dismounted and began to attack Rico with his fists, smashing his face
with a hot, unbridled rage.

Yet after a few minutes, Fernandez
pulled Dan away from his victim, saving
Rico's life.

"No, Senor! We don't want to kill him,"
Fernandez said.

Dan shook Fernandez off but didn't continue his pounding of Juanita's attacker.

Instead, he grabbed Rico by the hair and
dragged him right out of the water. Next
he kicked him hard enough to knock him
flat on his face.

Juanita regained her wind before long, then stood over Rico to cuss him, his mother, his father, his brothers, his sisters, and even his dog. She kicked him once and spun away, going toward the buckboard that had been standing near the river.

"What about Rico?" Bernardo asked.

"Escort him off our land," Juanita said. "If you see him again, kill him!"

All this time, she hadn't so much as looked at Dan. Now she threw her laundry into the wagon and was aboard before she turned to him.

"Why are you here, gringo?"

Dan dumped a bootful of water out on the ground. "Always nice to be greeted so warmly."

"I asked you a question, gringo."

"You never let up, do you? You just keep throwing that gringo business up in my face."

"You are a gringo."

"Gringo is not exactly a flattering word, Senorita."

"I am not in a flattering mood. I was very nearly drowned a few minutes ago."

"If I'm not mistaken, I saved you from being drowned. Seems you might at least be cordial to me for that."

The girl took a deep breath, pushed her damp hair over her shoulders, and carefully put her hat on her head. "Why did you come? You said you would not help."

"Your brother escaped, didn't he?"

Now the light of suspicion glowed in the young woman's eyes. "You!"

"I'm not saying that Pepe won't still be hanged, but he has a fighting chance. He turned himself in at Stockdale to Judge Larsen. It'll take these boys here some time to get him extradited. Maybe there'll be a new trial in Stockdale."

A thoughtful frown knitted the girl's brow. "Maybe you should come to our hacienda. I may have misjudged you. If you rescued my brother from certain death, you must have some ideas about what to do next. My father will want to handle the money end of things."

"What I've done could get me a few years in prison, but I didn't risk that for money," Dan said.

"No? Then for what?"

"For you, Juanita. To win your favor."

"You have no chance of that, gringo. If that's your only reason for being here in El

Hueco, you may as well leave right now. This minute."

"You warm my soul with your friendliness, Juanita."

"And don't call me Juanita. I am not one of your women!"

Dan shook his head, walked over to his horse, and mounted. "You're right, Senorita. I'm tired of all this, tired of being a gringo. I might as well leave right now. This minute." He turned his horse toward town.

"The hacienda is not that way, gringo," she snapped.

But Dan didn't even look back. He put his heels to his horse and left her, her wagon, and her laundry in his dust.

CHAPTER SEVEN

Hernando Mestas listened to his daughter. She was like his right arm, the stronger of his two remaining children. There were times when he wished he hadn't put so much on her shoulders, given her so much responsibility. For too many burdens could make a person too hard.

"But I don't understand," he said at last. "Why didn't this man return here with you?"

"I don't know," Juanita said, but she colored noticeably. That wasn't like her.

"You say he released Pepe and sent him to a judge in Stockdale, where he might get a little protection. Maybe a new hearing or trial. You tell me that this man arrived at the river to knock Rico senseless and save your life. I hear words of praise on your lips, but the feeling behind those words is not warmth."

"He's a gringo, Father," Juanita said.

"And all gringos are bad?"

"It was a gringo who killed my mother. It was a gringo who told us that we only owned a small part of the land we have claimed for years. It is gringos who work for Martinez and kill our men and your sons. There can be no good in a race of men who only live for greed and killing."

"If you walk through a forest of trees, you will see many that grow tall and straight. You would notice some were small and weak, some were crooked and rotted away. And there would be those that could not bend with a breeze. It is no different with a race of people. Some are tall and straight, even though they have small stature. There are crooked and rotten people in every race. And you will find those that cannot bend with a wind.

"Also, I wish you could truly learn that no man is all bad. Nor is any man all good. I am strong in spirit, yet my body grows weak with age. You are strong in spirit, yet your heart is sometimes too hard. But enough of this preaching. What's bothering you, Juanita?"

"I don't want to talk about it, Father."

"You won't open your heart to me?"

"Well, it's this...gringo." She blushed once more. "He wants me!"

"You are a beautiful woman. There are many men who want you."

"But he's a gringo!"

Her father nodded. "I see."

"You couldn't. You don't understand!"

"And you, my dearest daughter, in your heart you find this man to your liking. That's it, isn't it?"

Juanita turned away, hiding her expression. "I know he saved my life and Pepe's, but he's so arrogant, so impossible. Anyway, I could never marry a gringo. Never!"

"Still, you could have brought him to the house."

"Well, I invited him, but he didn't want to come," Juanita said. "I guess he had other things to do."

"Did this gringo say where he was going?"

"No. He rode toward town, but that's all I know."

"I will ride into El Hueco tomorrow. Perhaps I can meet this man and find out more about Pepe."

"Colin is sure to start trouble, Papa. I

don't think it would be wise to go into town."

"It's my town, Juanita. I helped to build it into a town. I won't be kept out of my own town."

"Then I'll go with you."

"It may mean facing this terrible gringo once more."

"I'm not afraid of him," she said quickly, but she could not hide the rush of crimson that bathed her throat and cheeks yet again.

Dan hadn't finished his meal before a man with a star was shadowing his table. Dan ignored him for a time, but the man grew impatient. He pulled out a chair and sat down across from Dan.

"I must be losing my memory, Sheriff," Dan said easily. "I don't recall asking you to share my table."

"What's your game, Keen? Why are you in El Hueco?"

"Thanks for your concern, Abel. I'm fine," Dan said sarcastically. "How about you and the family?"

"I always figured you for a smart

mouth," the sheriff growled. "You always got away with everything. And because you wore a badge, it made it all legal."

"Some might look at it that way. Especially those really working on the wrong side of the law."

"You making some kind of accusation about me?" the sheriff asked.

"If the badge fits, pin it on, Abel Corman."

"Your arrival here confirms something I've suspected since Pepe got out of jail. You were responsible for his break."

"Got the wrong man, Sheriff. I'm as honest and law-abiding as you are." Dan grinned. "Who told you where I was?"

The sheriff jerked his head toward the saloon across the street. "A couple of old friends of yours are in town. Jeeter Prize and Gore Olson."

"It's really nice of those fellows to remember me. It's been over a year since I ran them out of Stockdale."

"Their story is that you were after the same man as them. You earned the bounty on that one."

"I took him alive. You ever hear of Jeeter or Gore doing that?"

"So let's stick to the original question, Keen. What are you doing in El Hueco?"

"Drifting," Dan said.

"Drifting to where?" the sheriff asked.

"I gave my horse his head. He hasn't told me where we're going to end up. It's a surprise. He enjoys surprising me."

"I'll give you a surprise, Keen. It'll be a surprise if you're alive in twenty-four hours! Once Martinez decides that you're the one who helped Pepe escape, he'll want you dead!"

"I don't recall admitting to helping anyone break jail. Are you giving me the same kind of trial that Pepe got?"

"We tried him fair and square!" Abel Corman said.

"Who sat on the jury?" Dan asked.

"Twelve men! That's all the law requires —or had you forgotten?"

"Twelve impartial men, Abel. I doubt that there are twelve people in all of El Hueco who aren't affected by the outcome of the war between Martinez and the Mestas family. Judge Larsen might not recognize a kangaroo court like that."

The man's face twisted. "What's Larsen got to do with anything?"

"I met Pepe on the road between here and Stockdale. I advised him to give himself up to the authorities. He decided not to return here, so I imagine he went on into Stockdale. That would put him under Judge Larsen."

"So that's your game, is it?" the sheriff said.

"My game? I'm not in this private war."

"You killed Clay Yorker!"

"He tried to shoot me when I escorted a young lady out of town. I was minding my own business at the time."

"That'll be the day. You aren't here by accident. You've come into this valley to side old man Mestas!"

"Never met the man, or Martinez either. I've got no part in their feud. Of course"— he narrowed his gaze at the paunchy sheriff—"if someone was to start pushing me, I might take a hand. I don't like being pushed."

"You're not hiding behind a badge anymore, Keen. If you get out of line in El Hueco, I'll lock you up. Want to stay healthy and in one piece? Then you'd better hoist yourself back onto your horse and get out."

"Thanks for the generous offer, Abel. I'll certainly keep it in mind."

Abel stood up, almost knocking his chair over. Then he stormed out of the cafe without a backward glance.

Dan wasn't afraid of the sheriff. But he seriously thought about leaving town. It was obvious that he'd never get to hold Juanita in his arms again. To her all gringos were the same—dirt under her feet!

Still, he'd said he would help Pepe. And a promise was a promise.

Pushing the plate away from the table, Dan paid for the meal and went over to his rented room. It was only a small room in an attic above the general store, but it was quiet and he was able to be alone with his thoughts.

The trouble was, his thoughts were mostly about that blasted senorita! He'd never met anyone like her, never tasted such kisses. But she was an impossible woman. Impossible! She would drive him crazy.

Maybe he'd better leave El Hueco, after all.

CHAPTER EIGHT

It hadn't been a restful night for Dan, and the breakfast didn't have much taste. Even after hours of contemplation, he hadn't decided what to do. Yet he was involved—like it or not—because he'd helped young Pepe escape.

Judge Larsen had warned Dan against doing such a thing, indicating that he wouldn't lift a finger to keep him from going to prison for his lawbreaking. But Dan had only wanted to seek justice for the Mexican youth. Well, now he was in it up to his neck.

Dan paid for the meal after leaving a good portion of it on his plate. He still hadn't made any decision. Upon stepping out into the bright morning sun, he was suddenly aware that a decision had been made for him. Jeeter Prize and Gore Olson were waiting for him.

"Long time no see, Keen," Jeeter drawled.

"You look a mite underdressed, not toting that badge," Olson added.

"Howdy, boys," Dan said easily, but his heart was beginning to pound.

He glanced around to see if there were any more of Martinez's men about. It was no surprise to spot Colin Wyatt across the street, a wicked curl to his lips.

"You don't look near so big without that star, Keen," Jeeter said. "I always heard what a big man you was!"

"Maybe we ought to see how tough you are, without the United States deputy marshal title backing you up!"

"Seems you boys got up in a surly mood this morning. What happened? Someone kick over the rock you crawled under for the night?"

Dan was ready, knowing there was no way to avert the fight. He ducked Jeeter's vicious right hand, sinking his own right fist into the man's middle. Next he slammed Jeeter with a quick left to the face. But then Olson entered the fracas, and Dan knew he was in trouble.

In fact, it wasn't a fight anymore, just a vicious beating. And Dan was on the wrong end of it. When he inevitably went down to his knees, a rope came out of nowhere to snake around his neck. He managed to get an arm into the noose, though, before he was suddenly jerked off the walk and found himself being dragged out of town behind a horse.

The road was rough with rocks and gravel. Twisting, rolling over, taking a terrible pounding in every part of his body, bouncing like a tin can in back of a carriage with newlyweds, Dan wondered if he'd still be alive when this endless journey was over.

He'd almost stopped caring when he slammed into some brush. There his battered body finally came to rest.

His eyes closed, his mind barely able to function, he felt the rope being pulled off him. He hadn't the strength to open his eyes, but he felt a man standing over him.

"You don't look so tough now, Keen. If you've got the guts, just come back into El Hueco. I'll give you a demonstration of my speed with my two guns." The man laughed, jamming a boot into Dan's middle.

With the last of his strength, Dan did manage to briefly pry his eyes open, after all. He glimpsed Colin Wyatt sauntering away. He would remember this little ride. If he ever managed to walk again, he would make the gunman pay. First, though, he had to survive this ordeal.

Ah, die, Keen, why don't you—make everyone happy, Dan thought to himself, his consciousness fading. Then the darkness claimed him completely, dragging him into its arms and shutting out the world.

Martinez sat his horse like a king, tall, erect, his chin high. In El Hueco he was a lord, a baron. At thirty-eight, he had power and wealth. He was not satisfied with what he had, however. He always wanted more.

"And what of Pepe?" he asked Colin Wyatt. "Anything new?"

"No. Like I told you before, he turned himself over to the law in Stockdale."

"And how is Senor Keen feeling today after his exciting ride in the country?"

"Probably wishes he was dead," Colin said.

"You should have killed Keen," Martinez sighed. "I don't like the idea of him still breathing our air."

"Might have been some trouble over that. We don't want any other deputy U.S. marshals down here. He might have some lawmen friends."

"If the chance affords itself again, kill him. You let me worry about any of Keen's friends. I want that troublemaker out of my hair."

"He has to recover first. Maybe he won't make it. Many a man dies from being dragged around by a horse. I gave him a real good ride, and that road is pretty hard."

"I'll leave him up to you, Wyatt. That's what you're being paid for," Martinez said.

"What about Pepe?"

Martinez shrugged. "It's a matter for the law now. If Corman can't get him back, we'll send a few witnesses over to testify against him. If there is another trial. A gringo court will find him guilty, providing a few of your kind are there to point a finger at him. In American courts, Mexicans are always in the wrong."

"Any move you want to make against Hernando Mestas?"

"Rico made a mess of what I had in mind. Let's wait a few days and see what happens. If you get bored, there are always extra cattle on the Mestas spread. You might drive off a few and sell them."

"I'll get Pancho and Bobby on that. The slaughterhouse down near the border can always take forty or fifty head."

The baron nodded his agreement. "It isn't much, but each little raid, every steer Mestas loses, hurts him. He will break soon. His men have mostly deserted him. Soon our goal will be attained."

Expecting to see the blackness of night, to feel the chill of the cool air, and to discover himself still in the brush, Dan was confounded to find that he was alone in a small room. He blinked against the dim light from a nearby lamp and began to turn his head to look around. He stopped at once, for streaks of pain lanced through his neck and shoulders.

Waiting for the pain to go away, Dan took a rough inventory of his condition. He found one eye swollen nearly shut and a bandage on his forehead. Luckily nothing seemed to be broken. Yet all over his body there were bad bruises and scrapes, covered with some kind of ointment.

"So you're awake, gringo," a familiar voice said.

With a great deal of effort, Dan managed to turn his head enough to see Juanita in the doorway, clad in a robe and nightgown.

He had to swallow to clear his raw throat. "Would have thought you'd left me on my own."

"It would have served you right," she said icily. "You're very stupid, picking a fight with three men—Colin Wyatt included!"

"I wasn't exactly given any choice, ma'am. Jeeter and Olson were waiting for me. It was fight or run."

"And the great Dan Keen would never run," she said cynically.

"Never covers a lot of time, Senorita. Give me a chance to do this over—I'll run."

For the first time since he'd met up with the little vixen, he saw the whisper of a sincere smile on her face.

"Fortunately for you, Father wanted to

see what kind of a man you are. We happened to find you a short time after you made your way out of town. At first we thought there was only a pile of bloodied clothes tossed off to the side of the road. Somehow, though, it wasn't much of a surprise to find you among them."

"I'm flattered that you even took the time to bring me here. Was that an act of compassion toward me, or just a way of irking Martinez?"

"Both," Juanita said.

"You don't flatter a man, do you?"

"We owe you a debt, gringo. Whatever else you are, you did save Pepe from hanging."

"Glad that I have some worth in this world, after all."

"This is his room," Juanita said, ignoring his comment. "You can feel free to stay with us until you are better. There was not much left of your clothes worth saving, but we managed to get some of your things from town. And your horse."

"Paying the debt in full, huh?"

"Yes," she said matter-of-factly. "Would you care for something to eat or drink? You haven't had anything since this morning."

"If it wouldn't be too much trouble, just something to drink."

She turned around at once, and Dan wondered if she would ever stop thinking of him as a gringo. Probably not, he decided.

CHAPTER NINE

The next day Dan briefly met Hernando Mestas. He'd somehow pictured a man tall and erect, vain and proud. But Hernando didn't quite fit that mold. Though his eyes shone with determination and the sparkle of youth, his shoulders were bowed with age, the wrinkles deep under his eyes. He thanked Dan for helping his children, then quickly left the room.

On the following day, the two men talked for a while.

"You are a man of iron to recover from such a beating so quickly," the silver-haired rancher said.

Dan was sitting on the porch now, fully dressed but aching from head to foot. He still squinted through one puffy eye and walked stiffly from the scrapes on his knees. His clothes hid most of the marks of the brutal dragging, but the burn on one side of his neck would leave a scar for as long as he lived.

"I won't impose on you and your daughter any longer than necessary, Mr. Mestas."

A knowing look came into the older man's face. "You are planning to leave El Hueco?"

"What would you do if you were in my place?"

"Run like a frightened fawn," Hernando admitted freely.

"I've faced some long odds in my time, but you've really managed to get overmatched in this feud. How did you let Martinez come in and take over the way he has?"

"Foolish errors," Hernando sighed. "I kept thinking he would be satisfied with what he had. He took half of my empire and was not happy with it. I should have been the one dissatisfied. It was my range, my lands that were invaded and taken away. How could I have understood such a voracious appetite?"

"And it cost you some of your sons."

"All of them, if Pepe cannot be saved. And also my wife. That is a terrible price to pay for a simple piece of land."

"Some ground is like that—expensive," Dan said. "Your family's been here for many years, haven't they?"

"Yes, for many years. And when gold was discovered, I was among the first to provide miners with meat. Mestas cattle saved many a mining camp from going hungry, and the prices were always reasonable."

"And you made a fortune," Dan said.

"A small one—enough to build up this rancho, this empire of cattle and riders. I once had two hundred men working for me. Now Martinez has half of my range, some farmers have moved in to till the soil, and I am backed into a corner to go broke or die. Strange cycle to go through in a lifetime, is it not?"

"There are laws to protect you."

"There is no law, for there is no one to enforce it," Hernando said. "Words on paper will not stop a bullet."

"How did you acquire such a hate for white men?" Dan asked.

"I have no such hate, Mr. Keen. It is my daughter who vents her anger on you. It isn't always rational, but sometimes she is not rational in a number of ways."

"What did you think of her coming to

Stockdale to hire a gunman?"

"I thought she was wasting her time. What man would be fool enough to go up against the likes of Colin Wyatt and the other guns Martinez has?"

"With Pepe in jail, I guess she was desperate enough to do about anything to save him."

"When my wife and sons, Carlos and Ruban, were killed, Juanita and Pepe became very close. Sometimes I feel she wishes she were a man, able to take a gun and avenge those deaths."

"If you had the money, you could hire an army and fight back. You said that you'd made a small fortune."

"Had and spent, my friend. It cost a great amount of money to run this rancho, and I've lost hundreds of cattle to rustlers in the past three years. I hired more men and still lost cattle. Sometimes I think many of those I hired were working for Martinez at the time. Now I have very few men. That Pancho Valdez was once on my payroll. Now he is one of Martinez's top men. I kind of doubt that his position on that place is accidental."

"What about the death of that farmer? Is

there any way to prove your son's innocence?"

"He was out with the herd. He has no alibi," Hernando said.

"And the only witnesses were men working for Martinez?"

"Those were the only ones to come forward. It would have been very dangerous for anyone to take a stand against Martinez."

"Meaning what?" Dan said.

"Meaning that there was a witness, but she did not speak."

"She?"

"Carla Pajecho was out walking with Lorenzo Hoya that night. Carla is what you might call a free spirit. She doesn't like chaperones."

"Then Carla was a witness against Pepe?"

"Oh, no. Pepe had a liking for Carla. She and he were good friends."

"She was scared off then," Dan said.

"Exactly. I would gladly reward her with five hundred dollars. But Martinez plays very rough, and he has men on his payroll like Rico Lucinda. You recall the treatment Rico gave my daughter. And Carla has no one at all to stand at her side. My promises to look after Carla would have been futile, and she is not a fool. Keeping her mouth shut was her only safeguard against someone like Rico."

"If you could get a U.S. marshal down here, he could take Carla's sworn deposition. It might make the difference in whether your son is convicted of murder in Stockdale or goes free."

"To testify for him, Carla would have to be testifying against Martinez and his men. I don't think she'd like that idea much."

"Then what do you intend to do, Mr. Mestas?"

He shrugged his thin, bowed shoulders and lowered his silver head. "I will pray that Martinez will one day be satisfied with what he has, without killing my son."

Dan watched the man turn and walk away. He had once been proud of what he'd accomplished in his life. Now life was only a burden to him.

"He is beaten into the dust." Juanita's voice came from behind Dan.

He turned to see her standing in the doorway of the house. She moved out to

watch her father cross the yard to a waiting horse, her eyes burning with frustration and anger.

"Maybe he has simply reached a conclusion. He knows this is a war he can't win.
There comes a time to realize your position
is hopeless."

"How full of enthusiasm you are. What a
fool I was to ever think that you could have
been a help to us!"

"Go out looking for a miracle, you're
bound to be disappointed, Juanita."

"I don't remember giving you permission
to call me by my first name, gringo!"

"Sorry about that, spitfire. Guess I've
just got no manners at all."

"How very true!" she snapped. "You dare
to call me a spitfire, to insult me every
chance you get. Then you have the audac-
ity to speak my name as if we were actually friends."

"I have no idea how to be friends with
you, Juanita," he said with a shake of his
head. "You hate me for being a gringo, and
that's something I can't change. I don't
know what else I can do to please you."

"Try dropping dead!"

He had to grin at that, for Juanita

sounded just like a child.

"I think I've figured it all out," Dan said quietly, getting to his feet.

"And what have you figured out, gringo?"

"I think you enjoyed kissing me," he told her lightly.

"What?" She was incredulous.

He took hold of her shoulders and pulled her toward him. "You can't fight nature, Juanita. Love knows no race, no bounds."

She kicked him then—so hard that he let out a howl of pain. It was also enough to make him let go of her shoulders.

"You're a fool, gringo. I hope Colin kills you."

Standing on one leg, braced against the front of the house, Dan rubbed his freshly bruised shin. He regarded the impossible spitfire with hard eyes.

"A woman can have spirit and behave like a lady, Juanita. You enjoy being a witch!" He stood up straight once more, looking down into the girl's smoldering eyes. "If I run into Colin Wyatt, I'll tell him that you're on his side. That ought to make him happy."

Then he was turning away, walking into

the house. He would gather his things together and get out. He could hardly move a muscle without hurting, but he wasn't going to stay in the same house with Juanita any longer.

CHAPTER TEN

The sun was warm as Juanita rode up to her father and two of their men. She was not very proud of what she had to tell him, especially since he looked upset.

"Something the matter, Papa?"

The old man tipped a head to the foreman of their ranch. "Fernandez has discovered that we lost another group of cattle. It's getting so the rustlers don't even bother to hide their tracks. They know we haven't got enough men to pursue them."

"How many this time?" Juanita asked.

"Maybe fifty head," Fernandez said. "We didn't get here in time to see anything but a distant cloud of dust. If we only had more men, we could run them down by dark. But two more men quit yesterday. We have only a few left to run the rancho. It isn't enough to watch over all of the cattle. Everyone's afraid of Martinez and Colin Wyatt. They don't want to die over a few head of cattle."

"I don't blame them," Mestas said regretfully. "I would like to provide them with safe jobs and a secure future. I have never hired a regular gunman. Perhaps I've been wrong all these years."

"What are your orders?" Fernandez asked.

"Drive the herd toward the base of the mountain. Pin them inside an area where you and the men can watch over them. Patrol the range to the river in pairs. We must stop any further loss of cattle until I can locate a buyer. If I have to, I'll sell all of the cattle and hire men to simply hold on to this land."

"It will break you," Fernandez said.

"Better to be broken after putting up a decent fight for what has been rightfully my family's for so many years. I won't just give up my rancho to the likes of that worthless, greedy Martinez."

The foreman and the other rider rode off to carry out the orders, while Hernando Mestas gave his attention to his daughter. He seemed to read what was in her eyes.

"So you drove Keen away?"

"He...he left," she admitted, feeling the rush of crimson to her face.

"I could have wished him to remain for a

time. He was a man of great strength and character. He gave me some little hope."

"They rode him out of town at the end of a rope, Papa. How could he have been all that much good to us?"

"You forget so soon, don't you? He killed Clay Yorker, he saved you from Rico. It was he who saved Pepe from the rope of the hangman. What more must the man do to impress you?"

"He wants to court me."

"A number of men want to court you. You are a beautiful young woman."

"I sometimes think beauty is a curse."

"Do you now?" the old man said with interest. "And what if you took a fancy to some young man? How would you go about getting him to notice you?"

"I don't know. That's kind of a silly question."

"Not really. You have been blessed with attractive features, my daughter. To pick your man, you have to only select from admirers. A woman with ordinary or unattractive looks must earn the attention of the man she wishes. How very easy it will be for you to find a proper suitor, compared to the chore facing a less fortunate woman."

"There is the other side of the coin, Papa. Men want me, but do they really want to even know me personally? How many of them only want me as something to show off—like a high-stepping horse?"

"There are men like that, too. You will have to choose your man with care. It will have to be someone who loves you for yourself."

"How can I know such a man?"

"He will be honest with you, knowing your faults, yet loving you in spite of them." He grinned. "Take, for instance, your temper."

"I've always had a temper. I try to control it."

"And you do...some of the time. I wonder if you try to keep in your rein with certain men, however."

"Meaning Dan Keen?" Juanita said.

"You seem more than a little short-tempered when it comes to him. I sometimes wonder if you really hate him the way you claim."

"He's arrogant and proud, always thinking he's right. I don't know how anyone could stand to be around him."

"I did not find him such a man...but men are often different with other men than they are with women. When I was young, some of my friends were rotten to their wives. I happened to like them, but they deserved contempt for their attitude toward women. Strange, isn't it?"

"I suppose things are always like that," Juanita said. "I've met a few girls who used men as well. They only wanted what they could get from a man, never considering the man as a real person."

"And do you consider Dan Keen a real person? What do you truly think of him?"

"I have no feelings for Dan Keen—except for contempt!"

"You are quite sure?"

"Yes!" Juanita snapped.

"And why does he infuriate you so?"

"Because—"

"Why do you grow angry at the mere mention of his name?"

"Papa, I—"

"Why did you drive him away from our ranch if you weren't afraid to constantly be around him?"

"You're being foolish!"

"Perhaps," he admitted freely. Then he smiled. "And perhaps you don't really hate the gringo as much as you'd like to pretend."

Juanita jerked the reins of her horse, spinning him about. She put her heels to him at once, driving him away from the words that followed. She wasn't certain, but she thought her father was saying something about falling in love.

She clenched her teeth tightly, the tears burning at her eyes. What was the matter with everyone? Why did they believe she had to like Dan Keen? He believed it, her father believed it. Probably the stupid horse under her believed it!

"It doesn't matter now," she said tightly. "He's gone! He's left El Hueco! He's out of my life forever!"

But that thought didn't console her at all.

Never a man to quit a job, Dan made his way quietly into town and discreetly learned where he could find the girl, Carla Pajecho. He managed to slip into her small cabin without being seen. Then he sat back and waited for her to come home.

It was quite late when she finally arrived. She had been drinking, but she wasn't drunk. She didn't even flinch at finding Dan in her cabin when she lit a lamp.

"What do you want, gringo?" she asked wearily.

"I've been wanting to meet you, Carla," he said.

"So you've met me. What else do you want?"

"I've been waiting quite a spell. Hope you don't mind, but I looked around some."

"Ain't much to look at," Carla said.

"You've got some nice clothes. Do men often buy clothes for you?"

"I make all my own clothes," she said with a bit of pride. "I even do mending and sewing for some of the other folks in town."

"I'll bet you could run a profitable sewing or clothing business of your own. How'd you like to have a dress shop somewhere?"

The woman's eyes narrowed. "Who are you?"

"That isn't important, but what I have to say might be."

"So say it," she said.

"I've heard that you're a free spirit, Carla. Yet I bet you'd like to get married and raise a family. Maybe they think you're a little too wild here in El Hueco. But if you were to move away and start your own dress shop, you'd have dozens of bachelors trying to win your hand."

The woman's eyes lit up at that notion. "So what have you got in mind? I don't hold with breaking any laws."

"Good. Because all you have to do is uphold the law to earn that store and respectable position."

"Oh? How?" Carla asked sarcastically.

"I happen to know that you witnessed the killing of that farmer that Pepe Mestas was accused of murdering."

"Maybe," she said.

"It might interest you to know that Pepe is going to get a new trial in Stockdale in a few days."

"So?"

"So old man Mestas has offered a five-hundred-dollar reward for the arrest and conviction of the man or men who actually did the killing. I think you'd do quite well with that five hundred dollars."

The woman frowned. "I know who you

are now. You're that gringo that has been helping the Mestas family."

"I was, but I'm riding out. I'm not any match for Colin Wyatt."

"You just asked me to stick my neck out. Colin would chop my head off if he learned what I was up to."

"You'd have protection until you testified. After that, it wouldn't matter to anyone that you'd come forward. You could take a stage to anyplace you wanted and start over."

"This protection? It would come from you?"

"I'm heading in that direction. Once you get to Stockdale, Judge Larsen would have charge of your safety. He takes his job seriously, though. You'd be all right."

"And I'd get five hundred dollars?"

"You only have to point the finger at the man or men who really killed that farmer."

"I own a horse. Would you go get him from the stable, while I pack a few things?"

"You want to leave right now?"

"The sooner, the better, Keen. I've got a friend, and I'll tell her I'm going. Wouldn't want anyone thinking you kidnapped me."

"I'll second that motion."

"Hurry then. I might sober up completely and change my mind at any minute."

CHAPTER ELEVEN

Judge Larsen looked hard at Pepe, then glanced around the courtroom. His eyes rested for the briefest span of time on Dan, then fell to the papers on his desk.

"After reviewing the notes sent up from El Hueco, I find that Judge Dick Haller was functioning without proper authority. His position as justice of the peace does not give him judicial power in a murder case. And after considering the testimony of Miss Pajecho, and studying all of the relevant material, I hereby find the defendant, Pepe Mestas, innocent."

Hernando pushed forward at once to embrace his son, both of them shedding tears of joy. Juanita was more restrained, but she did take Carla's hand and thank her for coming forward. Dan noticed the way Carla nodded toward him, yet he quickly looked away. He would have left the room, but the town deputy took hold of his arm.

"Judge Larsen would like a few words with you, Keen."

"Right now?" Dan asked.

"Seems a good time. He's in his chambers."

Dan made his way to the small informal office behind the courtroom. Judge Larsen was already out of his robe. He poured two mugs of coffee from a pot that had been simmering on a potbellied stove and handed one to Dan.

"Some question might have come up about the reward money Carla received from Hernando Mestas, Keen. It might even look like a bribe to some people."

"I suppose so," Dan said.

"How did you know that I wouldn't look at it exactly that way?"

"You are very thorough, Judge. I figured you would talk to Pepe and then to Carla. You'd know that the boy wasn't a killer, and you'd have seen that Carla was telling the truth."

"You've been busy since I had your badge removed," Larsen said.

"El Hueco is a good place to find trouble, no matter what your motives, Judge."

"You hear about Brannigan?"

"No. What about him?" Dan asked.

"He was killed two days ago."

"That's a shame. Brannigan was a good man."

"It leaves me shorthanded as all get out, Keen. I haven't found a replacement for you yet."

"Life can be tough, Judge," Dan told him sarcastically. "Take me, a lawman without a star."

"I could remedy that."

"You took it—remember?"

"I've got a job that deserves some of your special skills," the judge said. "After reviewing the situation, I've come to the conclusion that you might be the only man for the job."

"That means that I'm expendable," Dan said.

"You're still sharp of wit, Keen. How about handling your gun?"

"I've kept up my practice—kind of an old habit I can't break."

"How'd you like to be a lawman again?"

"I'm between jobs right now. What's your angle?"

"There's some trouble down in El Hueco. I think a deputy U.S. marshal might be just the thing to put an end to it."

"Just as I thought. I'm expendable."

"Colin Wyatt doesn't have any outstanding warrants in California, but Carla pointed a finger straight at Pancho Valdez. I expect him to be brought to trial for murder."

"What about the range war?" Dan asked.

"See what can be done to bring it to a peaceful and bloodless end. I don't want a report on my desk in a week that contains a dozen killings. There has to be a way to deal out justice without all that shooting."

"Tall order, Judge. With Colin Wyatt in the game, I don't like the odds."

"I'm sorry on that count, but I haven't got the men to send with you. Do you want the job or not?"

"I'll take it, but I won't make any promises about gunplay. If my life is on the line, I'll use my gun. That's all there is to it."

The judge said, "No one expects you to get killed in the line of duty, Keen. I only ask that you try real hard to avoid bloodshed."

"It pains me to tell you this, Judge, but that's exactly the way I've always worked at my job. But men heading for a hanging don't feel they've got anything to lose in trying to kill me. In their place, I might feel the same way."

The judge picked up a piece of paper and a badge. "Here you go, Daniel Keen. I deputize you once more to do the job you're paid to do. This warrant is for Pancho Valdez. Serve it properly and bring the man before me."

"Martinez might have something to say about that."

"I know you'll do your best," Larsen said.

"That's a real vote of confidence from you, Judge."

"Maybe you impressed me by working so hard to save the life of this Mexican boy, Pepe. I'd always pictured you as only thinking of yourself. Well, word gets around. I know how tough this job was for you, and you didn't make a cent for your efforts. That says something for you that I'd never have suspected."

"Didn't know I was a humanitarian, huh?" Dan said.

"Never suspected it for a minute."

"Thanks, Judge. I'll be seeing you."

"I hope so, Keen. I hope your luck holds out."

* * *

Dan was alone in the Stockdale livery stable, saddling his horse, when he heard the approach of footsteps behind him. His hand dropped to his gun at once, but a glance told him he was in no life-threatening danger. His visitor was none other than Juanita Mestas.

For a change there was no look of anger or hostility on her face. She appeared almost embarrassed.

"Senorita Mestas," he greeted her carefully. "What brings you to the stable?"

She didn't answer at once. She took a moment to look Dan's horse over, noting the war bag, the fact that it was loaded down for a journey of some kind.

"You are leaving Stockdale?" she finally asked.

"Nothing more for me to do here. I was kind of looking after Carla, but she'll be on the stage out of town this afternoon. Judge Larsen has the local authorities making sure no harm comes to her. Something tells me she'll do just fine when she starts that dress shop of hers."

"Why did you waste the time to urge her to testify? I thought you had left El Hueco and all of its troubles behind you."

"I'm not the sort of man to start something and then not finish it. Pepe was still in jail, and he might have been judged guilty. I wanted justice done for his sake."

"We are again in your debt," Juanita said. "It seems we can't keep from owing you. What will it take for us to ever be on even terms?"

"Can't stand the thought of being indebted to me, can you?" Dan said.

The fire leapt into the girl's eyes. "No! What do you want of us?"

"What if I told you that a single kiss would make us even?"

Juanita struggled with that, her temper and her gratitude having a private war within her. "Surely there must be something else you'd rather have."

"No, Senorita. For one sweet kiss, I'll consider myself paid in full. In fact, I'll forget that I even know your name. If ever I set eyes on you again, I'll pretend that we never met."

Juanita didn't want to give in, not even with such a promise on his lips. She fought hard to control herself, to remain composed.

"That is a promise?" she said.

"You have my word."

She took a very deep breath, then clenched her fists. "Very well, gringo. You can kiss me, but only once."

Dan shook his head. "You have to do the kissing, not me."

"What?" She was incredulous.

"It is you who are paying a debt. I'm accepting one kiss as payment for a lot of trouble. The least you can do is make the effort and pay me in full. Of course, I'll expect you to kiss me as if you mean it."

"You go too far!" Juanita snapped. "How dare you expect me to actually kiss you!"

"Then we have no deal. I'm a man of my word. I thought your word would at least be as good as that of a gringo."

"All right! Blast your arrogance! I'll kiss you one time...just one time! Then we'll be even. You'll never again speak to me or darken my life with your presence!"

"I'll do my best to avoid you, Senorita. I've given you my word on that."

Juanita came closer to him then, as if anxious to get it over with. She had to stand on her toes to reach him, but his arms went around her at once. He helped by leaning down a bit to meet her, firmly placing his lips on hers.

Dan would never forget that kiss. It was as if all the frustration and fury in her was channeled into her lips, while her heart pounded and pounded. Then the fury was replaced by some other feeling. A warm feeling. Or was Dan imagining it?

Juanita seemed to pull away reluctantly, an odd look in her eyes. "There," she gasped. "We ... we're even."

"So we are, Senorita Mestas. You owe me nothing more for your brother's life."

"Very well," she said huskily. "Good-by to you forever, Dan Keen."

When Juanita was gone, Dan turned to his horse. "Tell me, you mangy critter. Did you ever see a woman who could kiss like that?"

The horse pushed his nose toward Dan for sugar or petting.

"You've got to be kidding, critter. There's no way you'd ever replace that spitfire, no way at all."

CHAPTER TWELVE

"It's a victory for them, boss," Colin said to Roberto Martinez.

"Yes. That Keen has been nothing but trouble to us. He has saved the Mestas boy and put Pancho's name on a wanted poster. He almost killed Rico, and he did kill Clay. I don't think I like that man mixing in my life."

"No reason for him to come back here. Jeeter was in Stockdale for the trial. He heard that Mestas had paid Keen in full."

"I didn't know the old man had so much money. He paid a reward to Carla for blabbing about Pancho, and he still had enough to pay off a man like Keen."

"I'd think a man of Keen's talents wouldn't come cheap," Colin put in. "How much do you think he got for saving Pepe?"

"Had to be more than Carla got for talking," Martinez said.

"What's our next move, boss? The Mestas

cattle are all being held at the base of the mountain in a box canyon. We can't get to them, and every man on Mestas's payroll is over there guarding them."

"How much grazing is available for his cattle?" Martinez asked.

"Maybe enough for a month. You want us to sit by and be idle for a month—wait him out?"

"I'm tired of waiting, Colin. For three years now, I've been waiting. I hired you to get me the entire valley. It's up to you to do what you were paid to do."

"That could mean an all-out war, boss. I've got Bobby, Rico, Jeeter, Gore, and Lorenzo, too. That's only a half dozen men. Even cut down, Mestas has about fifteen men guarding his cattle."

"You can easily cut the odds," Martinez said thoughtfully, "or perhaps another measure would send most of them running. Pepe got a reprieve from the hangman's noose, but a bullet knows no such charity."

"Pushing Pepe into a gunfight wouldn't be an easy chore. The boy is only seventeen or so. I don't think I've even seen him ever use a gun."

"I'm sure you can find a way to manage

things, to threaten Pepe. Even if he doesn't fight, you can make the old man think twice about hanging on to that damn land."

"You might have something at that, boss. Or maybe Pancho could kill Pepe and then leave for Mexico. If any lawmen come snooping, the trail would lead to the border. They'd have no reason to stick around and poke into our business in the valley."

"See what you can do, Colin. And don't take all year."

Colin Wyatt nodded and left the big house. Outside, several of his men were waiting.

"What's the deal, Wyatt?" Rico wanted to know at once.

"Got some action?" Bobby asked.

"Time's come to earn our keep, boys. We've been sitting idle since we railroaded Pepe into jail. Martinez is getting impatient. He wants the whole valley, and he wants it now." Colin turned to Valdez. "Get yourself some provisions, Pancho. After we do a little job in town, you'll be going to visit some of your kin across the border."

"That suits me, Wyatt. I don't like seeing

my face on a wanted poster."

"Gather your horses, boys. We've got work to do."

Dan had slipped into El Hueco under the cover of darkness, putting up his own horse. He spent the night in the livery loft and made himself scarce in the early-morning hours. He intended to have a few words with the good sheriff, but the jail was empty, and there was no sign of Abel Corman.

Everyone in town knew about Dan's bumpy ride at the end of Colin Wyatt's rope. When they saw him now with a badge on his vest, their eyes filled with curiosity.

He'd just discovered that Abel Corman had left town to do some fishing or hunting in the nearby hills when he turned his head and found himself facing Juanita Mestas.

"Pardon, Senorita," Dan said quickly and hurried into the saloon to get away from her.

Juanita surely felt that he'd deceived her in Stockdale by not telling her he was going back to El Hueco. Well, there was nothing he could do about that now.

"Drink, Mr. Keen?" the bartender asked. "I ain't open for business yet, but I'll certainly set you up."

"I'm not much of a drinking man, but I think I'll have a beer. If I'm not mistaken, I'll be needing it."

Juanita stormed into the general store, glaring at the middle-aged clerk. "That was Dan Keen!" she snapped, while Pepe walked in behind her.

The clerk could only shake her head affirmatively. She knew all about Juanita's hot temper and didn't want to add any fuel to it.

"How about that?" Pepe said cheerfully. "And he's wearing a badge again!"

"What?" Juanita spun on Pepe. "What did you say?"

"There's a star on his chest. United States deputy marshal, that's what he is."

"Why, that pompous, arrogant, lying sneak!"

"Whoa, sis! What put the cactus in your blanket?"

"Did you hear him speak to me out there?"

"No. I was tying up the horse when I spotted him."

"He acted as if he didn't even know me. The nerve of that . . . that gringo!"

"Maybe he didn't recognize you," Pepe said.

"Don't be stupid! Of course, he recognized me. He was just being impertinent. He made a fool of me in Stockdale, and now he's come to laugh at me!"

"I really don't think his wearing a badge and returning to El Hueco is spiteful toward you, Juanita. The judge promised he would send one of his men to investigate the trouble here. And he chose Dan for the job."

"That's no excuse. I'll bet Dan already knew he was coming here when he . . . when . . ." She reddened. "When I last saw him," she finally added.

"Why should it bother you so much?" Pepe asked. "Why make such a fuss?"

"He insulted me, Pepe. He purposely pretended not to even recognize me."

"I thought you said something about a promise he made you in Stockdale not to see you again. You told me that you'd put him out of your life for good. Maybe he was only keeping his word."

That slowed Juanita down. "Maybe you're right. I should have ignored him right off, pretended not to know him either. It was just the shock of seeing him here. I never expected to see him again."

"If he's come to investigate the trouble here, he won't be living much longer. Soon you won't even have to worry about avoiding him or ignoring him."

"That's a horrible thing to say, Pepe."

He grinned, and she knew at once he'd been teasing her. "Maybe you don't hate the gringo as much as you've been claiming, Juanita."

"But I do hate him!"

"Sure," he said with a snicker. "That's why it makes you so angry that he ignored you."

"That was just—he didn't have to be so rude!"

Pepe's knowing laugh was so infectious that Juanita had to join in.

"I'll be ready for him the next time," she managed at last. "I'll ignore him first!"

CHAPTER THIRTEEN

Dan saw trouble approach. He'd been sipping on the cool beer and looking out the window as Bobby Leets and Pancho Valdez rode up. They spotted the Mestas buckboard and tied off their horses next to it. Then Bobby headed down the street and into the shadows. Pancho took up a position just outside the general store. He had his gun loose in its holster, a hand nervously lifting it time and again.

"There another way out of here?" Dan asked the bartender.

"Beyond that corner table. Puts you in the alleyway."

Dan dropped a coin for the beer and hurried out the side exit. He then walked behind a few buildings, returned to the main street, and ended up in back of Bobby Leets.

Bobby had his gun out. Whatever trouble Pancho started, Bobby was there to back him up.

Dan pulled out his own gun just as Pepe and Juanita came out of the general store across the street. When they were stopped by Pancho, Dan clubbed Bobby with the butt of his gun, knocking him cold.

"I'm taking your sister with me, Pepe," Pancho was saying as Dan moved up behind him. "You can stop me with that gun you're wearing."

"No, Pepe!" Juanita cried, trying to step between the two of them.

Pancho gave her a hard slap, knocking her down near Dan. But the deputy marshal didn't have time to be a gentleman.

"You're under arrest, Pancho Valdez! Drop your gun!"

Pancho swung to face Dan, his hand drawing his pistol. It was not a smart move, for Dan already had his own gun. He only had to aim and pull the trigger.

The bullet took Pancho high in his right shoulder, knocking his gun out of his hand, making him stagger back like a drunk.

Dan rushed over to retrieve the gun before the man could recover. Then he grabbed Pancho by the neck and helped hold him steady.

"I'm arresting you for murder, Pancho.

Give me any trouble, and you can bleed to death!"

Pancho had his teeth clenched from the pain in his shoulder. His left hand was over the front wound, stopping the bleeding as best it could.

"Colin Wyatt will kill you, Keen. He'll gut-shoot you and let you squirm in the dust! That's when I'll walk up and spit in your face!"

"Gives me something to look forward to, doesn't it?"

Pepe gave his sister a hand up, then walked over to Dan. He put his hand down to his own pistol and shook his head.

"My gun wasn't even cocked. He would have killed me for sure. This makes it twice that I owe you my life."

Dan couldn't help but glance at Juanita. She was rubbing a red blotch on her cheek, evidence of the brutal wallop she'd taken from Pancho. She carefully avoided eye contact with him.

"Just once, Pepe," Dan said with a sly twist of his lips. "I was paid in full for helping you the first time."

Juanita bit her lip, lowering her head with something akin to embarrassment.

She had nothing to say, not even a "drop dead, gringo."

"Let's move, Pancho," Dan said, giving his prisoner a shove toward the jail. "Corman took a fine day to go fishing, but the catch of the week is going to be sitting in his cell come nightfall."

"I'm bleeding, Keen. I need a doctor."

"Did you get a doctor for that farmer you killed?"

"Weren't no need of a doctor for him. I'm a better shot than you are."

"Hardly that. I didn't kill you on purpose. You'll have to stand trial and hang."

"It's a long way to Stockdale from here, Keen. Once Wyatt learns that you're in town, your life won't be worth two cents."

Dan gave Pancho another push, forcing him down the walk. He heard Pepe say something about sending the doctor, but he was already on the alert for more trouble.

Bobby Leets was up on his feet, rubbing the back of his head. He wasn't the kind of man to face another with a gun. He only glared across the street. By the time Dan had made his way to the newly rebuilt jail, Bobby was on his horse, heading back to the Martinez ranch.

The old doctor arrived at the sheriff's office a few minutes later. He cleaned and bandaged the wound for Pancho, then accepted some money for his trouble and left. It wasn't long before Dan had two more visitors—Pepe and Juanita.

Pepe stood near the window and looked out into the street. "What will you do, Dan? Wyatt will be coming for you soon. They can't let you take Pancho before a judge. He just might say Martinez was behind the killing of Jake Blair."

"Martinez is already suspect, Pepe. I intend to have a talk with him. If it warrants, I'll arrest him."

"You have such a high opinion of yourself, gringo!" Juanita said.

Dan grinned, enjoying the feast of her beauty before his eyes. "I don't believe I know you, Senorita. Did you have something to say to me?"

"Don't play your stupid games, Dan Keen! You've set yourself up as a target. Take Pancho and ride for Stockdale. Maybe you can make it before Wyatt catches up with you!"

"I gave my word not to talk to you again,

Senorita Mestas. Are you releasing me from that promise?"

"Your promise was a lie!" she snapped.

"Did I say that I'd never see you again? I just said I'd pretend not to recognize you if we passed in the street. Did I break that word?"

"You lied! You told me that you'd never trouble us again, that you'd leave me alone!"

"I've made no attempt to be with you, Senorita. I didn't drag you to this jail. It's you who've come to me."

"That's got nothing to do with anything! You knew you were coming back to El Hueco. You knew that you'd see me again! You tricked me!"

"It's lucky for me that he did," Pepe put in. "Pancho would have surely killed me out there in the street."

"No one asked you to butt in, Pepe!" Juanita flared at her brother. "Keep your blasted gratitude to yourself!"

"Your sister certainly has a temper, Pepe. Has she always been such a spitfire?"

Pepe nodded. "Since she was just a child she was explosive and easily angered. I

don't think she would make much of a wife.
A man could never get along with her."

"You could have a point there, Pepe. A
man would have to get used to her temper,
to kind of work his way around it."

"You two idiots!" Juanita cried. "You
talk such nonsense! What will you do about
Wyatt? Amuse him with your silly chatter?"

"My sister could have a point, Dan. Do
you have a plan of some kind?"

"Concerning your sister, no. I guess
that'll take a lot more thinking than I've
got time for right now. As far as Wyatt
goes, I'll have to start out by trying to stay
alive."

"That won't be easy. If you'll have me, I'll
stand at your side."

"You're not exactly a gunhand, Pepe."

"I could use a shotgun. I'd be more help
than Abel Corman."

"No! I won't hear of it!" Juanita snapped.
"You're coming home with me. Papa would
die of a heart attack if he heard you've
joined this gringo against Wyatt and his
killers!"

"I can't just stand by and let Dan fight

our battles for us and not even try to help. This is our war, dear sister. If I can be of any help, I'm glad to do it."

"But, Pepe—"

"Take the supplies home and tell Papa what happened. I know he'll understand."

The girl sighed in defeat. "I'll tell him that you chose to die with the gringo. If he understands that, I hope he explains it to me so that it makes sense."

"Maybe he'll send Bernardo and Fernandez to help us. Tell him the time has come to finish our war."

Juanita didn't look at her brother. Instead, she focused her hot, smoldering eyes on Dan.

"Maybe you didn't do us any favor by saving Pepe from hanging. I'm afraid he'll be killed at your side. So I can't tell if your coming here is a blessing or a curse."

"Only time will tell that, I suppose," Dan said.

"Why did you come back here? You've already admitted that you're no match for Colin Wyatt."

"Situations change, Senorita Mestas. The last time I saw you in Stockdale I knew some things are worth dying for."

A wave of confusion flooded Juanita's face. Her expression grew soft, then hardened again.

"You promised to stay out of my life," she reminded him.

"And I will. The judge only sent me here to bring Pancho to trial."

"And what about me?" Juanita asked.

"I just said I'll stay out of your life."

"And never forget that, gringo!" Tossing her silky black hair over her shoulder, she left the two men in the office.

Pepe waited until Juanita was out of earshot before he told Dan, "I've never seen my sister act the way she does with you. Never!"

"What did I do to deserve it?"

"I think she' falling in love with you," Pepe said bluntly. "But she's fighting it with every breath she takes."

"That's the kind of thing that can drive a man crazy, Pepe."

"And you? Are you in love with my sister?"

"That's a very personal question."

"Look, Dan, you've saved my life twice. I

think that gives me the freedom to speak to you as a close friend."

"I think your sister is more than I could handle, Pepe," Dan sighed. "I'll never be anything to her but a gringo. Tough to fight that kind of thing."

"Her anger has grown worse since she was a child. It was bad enough when the white kids called us names at school. But when our mother and brothers were killed by white men, Juanita vowed never to forget that. She's afraid of being disloyal to their memory."

"Then why don't you hold their death against me?" Dan said.

"I don't have to worry about you in the same way," Pepe said with a wide grin. "I'm not afraid of falling in love with you."

"Now that's a relief," Dan laughed.

"But you see what I mean, don't you?"

"What you're saying is that she hates me more each time she finds herself liking me for something."

"Exactly. She had to fight a war inside herself all the time. The more she likes you, the more she tries to hate you."

Dan shook his head in defeat. "Maybe we

ought to worry about Colin Wyatt instead
of trying to understand that sister of
yours."

"You give the orders, Keen. I'll follow
them."

CHAPTER FOURTEEN

Abel Cormen cleaned out his desk with the haste of a man who was desperate to leave town. He hardly spoke a word, throwing his badge on the floor, then gathering up his things. He had been a pawn for Martinez. And now that the real law had arrived at El Hueco, he just had to get away.

Before leaving, he paused at the door.

"Your time is up, Keen," he sneered. "You'll play the high gun for a day or two, but Colin Wyatt is going to put an end to you."

"What are you going to do now, Corman?"

"Join the winning team, Deputy. It might even be my bullet that puts an end to your life. That has a nice ring to it, don't you think?"

Dan said, "If you're man enough, why not try it to my face? Martinez would likely give you a fat reward for killing me."

123

But Corman was having none of that. "I'm not a fool, Keen. Why take a chance against you on a one-to-one basis? Soon it'll be twenty or more against just you. If I have to wait my turn to put a bullet in you, I guess I can have that much patience."

"You're a real man's man, Corman. Bet your mother is real proud of the way you've turned out."

The ex-sheriff didn't reply. He just took his gear out of the jail, mounted his horse, and rode off in the direction of the Martinez spread. Dan had the distinct impression that he would have been wise to force the man into a fight. It would have been one less to face later.

Pepe came out of the darkness, a shotgun in his hands. He tried to hide the fear he felt, but it shone in the pale complexion, in the wide eyes and damp brow.

"You think they'll hit us tonight?"

"I doubt it. Look, maybe you should leave town, after all. You might as well ride out to the ranch and see how things are there. I'll stick it out with Pancho tonight."

"If you say so."

"Just don't take the main trails. No telling what Martinez will do, but it's bound to be deadly. He might just order you killed outright—your pa too."

"I'll tell Pa and everyone to be careful."

"Just so long as the ranch keeps up its own defense. Wouldn't be much to fight for if all of you got yourselves killed."

"I hear you talking, Keen, and I'll be careful. See you early tomorrow morning."

"So long, Pepe, and thanks for sticking by me."

Dan glanced at the cell. His prisoner was asleep on his bed, almost as if he hadn't a care in the world. Was he that sure that his friends would help him?

Looking around his new temporary home, Dan barred the door. A cot was on one side of the room, the desk on the other, with a potbellied stove in the middle of the floor. Dan decided to get some sleep. He didn't really expect Martinez to formulate any major campaign until a day or two had passed. For he seemed to be a patient man.

All the same, Dan moved the cot next to the front wall, so he'd be better able to hear any boots on the outside walk. The small bed also barricaded the door that way.

It seemed his eyes had only closed for a

moment when the shock of an explosion knocked him right out of bed. Dan hit the floor with his gun in his hand, half dazed. A shadow loomed out of the dark, coming through the opening made by the dynamite explosion.

"Hold it!" Dan shouted.

The man's gun instantly fired in Dan's direction. He was outlined briefly in the flash of his gun, but ducked away before Dan could return the fire.

"You've got no chance!" another man snarled. "Turn Pancho loose and we'll ride off!"

"You want him—come get him!" Dan called back. "If I give him to you, he'll already be dead!"

It was fortunate that Dan was on the ground. For a barrage of bullets began to pelt the walls, some coming through the thin mortar. About six or seven guns seemed to be firing rapidly, shattering the night, destroying the walls of the jail.

Dan slid under the cot and tried to see through the dust and darkness within the room. He had no way to even move without risking death.

Pancho cried out once, but then he fell back. It sounded as though he'd been mortally wounded by several bullets. Apparently the gunmen had not come to safeguard Pancho's life, only to destroy the building and kill Dan Keen. Pancho had been expendable once the explosion had failed to kill Dan.

By moving his cot, Dan had staved off his own death for the moment. But lying on the floor, dirt in his mouth, dust in his eyes, he wondered just how long he'd managed to put off Mr. Death.

The gunfire continued for a full fifteen minutes that seemed like an eternity to Dan. He kept waiting for the one bullet that would get him. But none did.

When the shooting finally stopped, Dan found his ears ringing and the cloud of dust almost impenetrable. Everywhere there was debris from the shattered walls. It helped to hide Dan.

His gun was still cocked. And when a shadowy figure appeared at the same hole in the wall, Dan was able to hit him.

As if that was a signal, the guns opened up again. Then, when a second explosion brought down another wall, Dan found himself nearly buried under rock and rafters.

The bullets didn't stop until a third explosion jarred the earth. This time the entire building was leveled, raising an enormous cloud of dust and smoke.

Dan, still trapped by debris, was unable to move. He wasn't even able to use his gun. When they discovered him, he would die.

And as he waited for his doom, he thought, Blast your beautiful hide, Juanita. This is one mess you've gotten me into—one hell of a mess!

Juanita was out of bed, rubbing the sleep from her eyes. She grabbed her robe and hurried into the living room. Pepe was already dressed, and her father was just putting on his second boot. Fernandez was at the door, dressed as if ready to ride.

"What is it? What's going on?" Juanita asked.

"Just go back to bed," her father said quietly. "Two men will be on guard outside."

"What happened? Did they raid our cattle again?"

"It's Keen," Pepe told her softly. "They've attacked the jail."

Juanita caught her breath, hurriedly turning her attention to Fernandez, who'd been watching the roads.

"What have they done? What about Dan?" she demanded.

"We don't know yet," her father replied. "Fernandez only learned from some rider that there were several explosions and gunfire."

"Si, Senorita," Fernandez said quickly. "Some men attacked the jail. There were two or three explosions, big booms, as if they blew up the entire place."

"And Dan?" she asked again. "What about him?"

"That's where we're going!" Pepe snapped, grabbing his shotgun. "If we don't get started, he'll be dead for sure."

"No one could be alive in that place, not with them dynamiting it that way," Fernandez remarked hopelessly.

Juanita ran to her room, pulling her clothes and boots on in no time. But the men had left before she went outside. To her dismay, there wasn't even a horse saddled. She had to get Bernardo to catch her a mount.

She paced like a caged animal, urging the ranch hand to hurry. He was as good with a rope as any man on the ranch, but he missed with his first loop and Juanita swore.

"Well, get on with it!" she shouted. "Hurry up! Dan might be dying at this very minute!"

Bernardo didn't miss his second throw, the rope settling neatly over a big mare's head. He worked almost feverishly to saddle the horse. Before he could even check the stirrups for length, Juanita was on the animal's back, racing out of the yard.

The other guard walked over to Bernardo. He shook his head, setting his rifle down next to his foot.

"She sure makes a fuss over a man she hates."

Bernardo nodded. "So eager she is just to watch a man die. You think you will ever marry, Paco?"

"If I do, it won't be to a woman like

Juanita. She is too much of a spitfire."

"It would be a challenge, Paco. She certainly would be a challenge."

CHAPTER FIFTEEN

Dan, still trapped in the rubble of the demolished sheriff's office, expected to die at any moment.

"Where the dickens is that coyote?" a voice rasped.

"Like trying to find a tick on a shaggy dog!" another complained. "I thought Corman said he slept next to that first wall we blew up."

"Corman ain't much help now. Keep digging! That sidewinder has got to be in here somewhere. If you so much as see his hat, we'll fill it full of lead."

"Don't have to tell me that twice. But with all that dynamite and gunfire, he's got to be dead."

"I want to see the body!"

Suddenly the two men stopped searching. Dan thought that they'd finally seen him. He got ready for the bullets that would kill him.

"Riders coming!" a new voice shouted.

"Looks like several men!"

"Mestas!" someone else cried. "Let's get out of here!"

Like scurrying rats, the two men left the rubble and made their way out to the street. Dan could hear the horses as several men rode out of town. He relaxed, unable to believe he was still alive.

The sound of approaching horses was music to Dan's ears. He recognized Pepe's anxious voice a few minutes later but waited for the youth to come closer before answering. For he didn't have much strength left.

"Where are you, Dan Keen? Answer me!"

"H-here!" Dan said at last in a strangely hoarse voice.

As the digging started, another horse came into town at a run. Within seconds, Dan heard Juanita's voice. She seemed genuinely concerned. It was a gratifying feeling, but it was somewhat muted due to the lack of air and the heavy load that Dan had supported for so long. Finally the load became too much, and he let himself drift into a painless oblivion.

* * *

When Dan next opened his eyes, Juanita was standing over him. He was in one of the hotel rooms, and it was full light outside. The girl had on an apron and held a damp cloth in her hands. He swallowed, trying to find his voice, while locking eyes with the little spitfire. He couldn't read what was hidden in the mysteries of her heart.

"Stupid gringo," she greeted him with her usual zest.

"Pancho?" he asked. "Is he dead?"

"He was shot to pieces. I can't believe that you escaped with only a few bruises. How do you lead such a charmed life?"

"Must be the kind of rewarding work I do."

She grunted. "According to the gossip—Martinez gossip—you were attacked by a couple of men last night. They were recognized by that Jeeter character as the Unger brothers. He said that you had killed one of their kin some time back."

"Good story," Dan said dryly.

"Abel Corman came to your rescue and was killed, the gossip goes. It isn't known if the Unger brothers killed him or if you might have shot him by mistake. He was found in the alley."

"If I killed him, it was no mistake."

"What about these Ungers?" Juanita asked.

"I killed an Unger last year in Cortez, but those weren't the Ungers last night. And there were more than two of them."

"Will that hold up in court?"

"I doubt it," Dan said.

"Then you can't prove that it wasn't the Ungers seeking revenge."

"That's about the size of it."

"Then you've failed. You may as well go back to Stockdale and tell the judge that you couldn't bring your man back alive. He'll likely assign you to another case."

"Is that what you want?" Dan asked.

Juanita didn't meet his eyes. She began to busy herself with the cloth and a pan of water. "It is of no concern to me."

"That why you rode into town last night like some kind of she-devil on wheels?"

That brought a blush to her cheeks. "I don't know what you're talking about. I came in to see if I could help—same as the rest of my family."

"I think you came in to see that I was all right."

Juanita glared at him. "You are so sure of yourself, aren't you? You think because I've been forced to kiss you that your charms have put me under some kind of spell."

"That'd be a fair turn of events. Your kiss sure enough put me under some kind of spell or curse."

"Curse?" she snapped. "What are you doing, calling me a witch?"

"Could be," he said with a grin. "You bewitched me from the time I first set eyes on you."

"How can I even stand to be in the same room with such a crazy, arrogant, self-centered gringo? Do me a favor and get out of my life!"

"Here you are, tending to me like a loving nurse, almost begging me to yip at your heels like a lovesick puppy. Then you go and spoil it all by calling me names."

"I'll do more than that," she said, dumping the pan of water right in Dan's face!

He coughed, sitting upright. He might have made a grab for Juanita, but she was quickly out of the room. He had the feeling that she wouldn't be back for a long time.

With no little effort, Dan managed to get out of bed. He was still wearing his trousers, but his shirt was gone. He stiffly shook out his muscles, testing the damage. He had darkish blotches all over his skin, but he figured he'd survive.

"That little hot pepper was right about one thing," he told his reflection in the mirror. "You were darned lucky to get out of that place with a whole hide." He kept staring at the mirror.

"Tell me, will I ever be lucky enough to get anyplace with Juanita? What do you think?"

"I think you're crazy for talking to me," the face in the mirror answered.

"Never get any help out of you, dummy," Dan grunted. "No help at all."

Hernando Mestas didn't hide his suspicions. He was eying Martinez with a close scrutiny. It was the first time the land baron had set foot in the Mestas house. Now he was standing in the middle of the living room, his sombrero in his hands. He had just made a very surprising suggestion to the older man.

"What do you have to say, Hernando?"

"You must forgive me, Mr. Martinez. I have not fully understood your proposal. What exactly is this merger you speak of?"

"A way to end the fighting between us. Look what it has done to both you and I. I am nearly broke from hiring these gringo gunfighters. You have lost a wife and two sons, while I have lost several good men and a great number of cattle. It is clear Pancho killed that farmer to make your son look guilty. If not for the intervention of that Keen, the boy would have been hanged for a crime he didn't commit."

"And you are willing to call a ceasefire to this war?" Hernando asked.

"More than that, Hernando. What I offer you is a part of all that I own."

"Perhaps you would explain it to me once more, a bit slower this time."

"Certainly," Martinez said easily. "Ours would be a kind of partnership. The two ranches would merge into one, with all of the cattle using the range and water together. We would share the land and share the rewards. I'm sure you must realize that I have several times the number of cattle you now own. But I would be willing to give you one-third as your share of the partnership. You don't have near that number of livestock, but I'm trying to be fair. Obviously, you have suffered greatly with this fighting. I want to put all that behind us."

"And what would I need to do?" the older man asked.

"Simply sign a contract. It would say you agree to share the land and water for one-third of the profit on our joint herds. The signing is necessary only so that Pepe will honor the contract when he assumes control of your interest."

"You surprise me with your generosity, Mr. Martinez."

"There is one condition."

"And what would that be?" the old rancher asked.

Martinez looked Hernando Mestas right in the eye. "I should like to marry your daughter, Juanita."

That took Hernando totally by surprise. "Surely you're joking, Mr. Martinez. Juanita would cut your throat on the night of your wedding."

"Let's be logical about this, Hernando. I have enough men to level this place and wipe you all out. If I turn Colin Wyatt—or one of his men—loose, he might even kill Juanita. At the very least, there is the possibility that a stray bullet would hit her. Wouldn't it be much better to see the killing stop?"

"You're asking the impossible, Martinez. I can't tell my daughter to marry you."

"I'm not such an old man, Hernando. I would make her a good husband. Our children would be your grandchildren. What better way could there be to put an end to this fighting?"

"She would never agree."

"What kind of man are you, Hernando? Have you forgotten the centuries of arranged marriages, the suitors picked by fathers for their daughters? Surely Juanita will obey you. I tell you, it is the only way to end the killing."

Hernando felt very old. He could not bear the thought of more killing. "I can't give you an answer this minute. I must have time to think, time to speak to my daughter."

"I promise you a truce then. One week, Hernando. You have one week to decide. If

Juanita refuses me, I can't be held responsible for the actions of Colin Wyatt. One
way or another, I'll put an end to this war.
Why not do it the peaceful way? It's up to
you to stop the bloodshed."

Even as Roberto Martinez left the room,
Hernando's mind was reeling. He knew the
younger man was not bluffing. This was
the final ultimatum before an all-out war
was declared.

Juanita happened to come into the room
a short time later. She had been busy at
the back of the house and not been aware
of any visitor. Hernando hadn't the courage
to look her in the eye. He couldn't ask her
to marry a man she truly hated.

"There has to be another way!" he
snapped harshly. "There has to!" He
paused. "But what if there isn't?"

"What's wrong, Papa? What's the matter?"

"I have a choice for you, my daughter,"
he sighed. "A very sad choice. But we have
been driven into a corner. We no longer
have the money to fight, nor the men to
resist Martinez. As I see it, we have but
two alternatives. One means a lot more

killing. And the other..." His voice broke.

"The other what? What are you talking about, Papa?"

He sighed deeply. "I'll explain, Juanita. I would rather take a beating, but I'll explain it all to you."

CHAPTER SIXTEEN

Colin Wyatt couldn't believe his ears. He was primed for a fight, ready to move in for the kill. Now Martinez was telling him to wait.

"It's just until the U.S. deputy marshal leaves El Hueco, Wyatt. I don't want to draw in the army against us. If we're patient, I think we can still get the entire valley."

"But you told me to get the boys ready. I've done a lot of saddle pounding lately. We're ready to strike at the cow camp and run off the rest of the Mestas cattle. That would break him right in two!"

"It would also give Dan Keen a reason to stick around. Don't you see the logic in this truce? Once Keen is gone, there'll be no witnesses to tell how we got the rest of the Mestas spread. If we attack now, we'll have to kill Keen. And that could bring a dozen marshals sniffing around."

"But marriage to that hellcat?" Colin said. "I can't believe you'd consider such a thing. She'll cut your throat the first chance she gets. That's one holy terror there."

"I know how to handle her," Martinez said.

"Wish I had your confidence, boss."

"You let me worry about Juanita. What I want now is for you and the boys to keep things quiet. It's got to become so peaceful in this valley that Keen'll be sent somewhere else."

"And if he doesn't go?" Colin asked.

"Then an accidental death might occur. Whatever takes place, we don't want a bunch of nosy marshals down here."

"You're the boss, but I hope you know what we're doing."

"Stick with me through this, Wyatt. You'll be ramrodding the biggest spread in these parts. One day soon you'll have the Mestas ranch as your own. You'd like that, wouldn't you?"

"You know I want to hang up my guns one day soon, boss."

Martinez said, "Then let me play the game by my rules. I tell you this'll work.

From all I've heard, Keen is calf-eyed over that little spitfire. Once she's married, he'll have a double reason for leaving El Hueco."

"Guess you're right about him and the girl. It's just that I never expected you to actually marry anybody. You're not the kind of guy to be tied to one woman."

"Marriages don't always last forever, Wyatt," Martinez said with a sly grin. "Sometime after I gain control of the Mestas spread, little Juanita just might have a terrible accident. I'll be so broken up about it that I'll probably mourn for her at least a week."

"Then find yourself another girl, huh?"

Martinez said, "You know me pretty well, Wyatt. I'm glad we're on the same side of the fence. I'd hate to have you on the other side."

"But is there a chance? Do you really think old man Mestas will give up Juanita's hand to end the fighting?"

"What are the choices open to him?" Martinez said with a shrug. "He either agrees or gets wiped out."

"Result is the same either way. I don't see you sharing this valley with Mestas."

"He's an old man, ready to die at any time. His son is reckless and will likely get himself killed within a few months."

"And that leaves only Juanita," Wyatt said.

"Exactly. When I tire of her..." Martinez shrugged.

"Then I have my foreman's ranch," Wyatt finished knowingly.

It was a hopeless task questioning the townspeople. No one had dared to stick his head out during the attack on the jail. Or so they all said. But several people repeated the fabricated rumor that the Unger brothers were trying to kill Dan, that they must have dynamited the jail and shot Pancho.

The Unger brothers were nowhere to be found, and there was no hard evidence to tie Martinez or Wyatt in with the business at the jail.

After several days of futile investigation, Dan was eating supper at the cafe, feeling frustrated. As he finished his bowl of stew, a tall, slender Mexican walked up to his table. He wore a well-fitting suit, his boots were polished to a high sheen, and his immaculate shirt appeared to be made of silk. He was striking, shoulders erect, hair neatly in place, an expensive sombrero in one hand.

"Would you mind if I joined you for a few minutes, Senor Keen?"

"You must be Martinez," Dan replied.

The man smiled, pulling out a chair and sitting down. "You are as I pictured you, Dan Keen, strong, sure of yourself, suspicious, and sharp of mind."

"I've been meaning to ride out your way, Martinez. There are some unanswered questions about Pancho—"

The newcomer held up his hand to silence the questions. "Pancho is behind us now. He was a wild hombre, always getting into trouble. I should have never hired such a man. I'm relieved that you discovered the truth of his guilt before it cost the innocent life of Pepe Mestas."

"Bet Pepe's hanging would have kept you awake nights feeling guilty," Dan retorted cynically.

"You seem to view me in a bad light, Senor Keen. I wish to put these suspicions of yours to rest. The war in this valley is over."

"How's that?"

"I and Hernando Mestas have come to terms. There will be no more fighting, no hostility between our men."

"Colin Wyatt isn't the kind of man to herd cattle. What are you going to do with him and the other gunmen?"

"I think you have a poor opinion of Wyatt. He wants to hang up his guns and lead an ordinary life. He's an adequate foreman. As for the others, I wouldn't have men like Jeeter Prize and Gore Olson on my payroll. I may let Rico and Bobby go as well. After all, I have many vaqueros, and Mestas has some men, too. Once our spreads are under a single ownership, there will not be such a need for riders."

That caused Dan to lift his eyebrows in surprise. "Single ownership?"

Martinez asked, "You haven't heard about our merger?"

"No."

"I'm sorry, Senor Keen. No wonder I made no sense to you." He smiled. "I'm going to marry Juanita. The ranches will be joined as one. There will be no more feuding between us."

"I see." Dan tried to cover his shock.

"Then you will also see that there is no need for you to continue to hound my men. There will be no more killing, no reason for you to stick around El Hueco."

"That would seem to be the case," Dan agreed.

Martinez stood up, a satisfied smile on his lips. "Fine, fine. I knew you were a reasonable man. It has been a pleasure meeting you, Senor Keen. Perhaps one day you will stop by our fair town again."

Dan watched the man leave the cafe. He walked with an arrogance to his stride, shoulders squared, nose high. Martinez had won.

Tossing some money on the table, Dan left the confines of the cafe. He went out into the dark, needing to get some fresh air, to be alone with his thoughts.

He avoided the saloon, walking a short distance from town. He found a large rock, amid some trees, sheltered from the cheerful sprinkling of stars that now shone overhead. He sat down to contemplate what he'd learned.

Juanita was going to marry Martinez! The thought was like a hammer, pounding into his head again and again. It didn't seem possible, but Martinez would not have lied about such a thing.

Something turned within Dan's chest, something jagged and rough. He had begun to have hopes for Juanita and himself. He'd thought that, despite her hatred, he would somehow win her over. But now she was forever out of reach.

The silence of the night numbed his spirit. The kisses he'd tasted, the feeling of her in his arms—that was all Dan would have to remember Juanita by. Martinez was right. There was no reason for him to remain in El Hueco.

CHAPTER SEVENTEEN

"It's the logical solution," Juanita said. "It will end the fighting. We are doomed to death unless we compromise."

Pepe regarded his sister as if her head was screwed on backward. "Compromise!" he cried. "Carlos died an agonizing death, shot down by Martinez's men! They shot Mama, too. Ruban survived for several days, until infection killed him in the most horrible way! What are you saying, Juanita? Have you lost all your sense?"

"Do you want to die?" she fired back. "Do you want to see Father killed as well? We have no choice!"

"I can't accept it. Such a sacrifice—no! If you marry Martinez, how can I hold my head up? How can you look at anyone you meet? That scum—it's impossible!"

"We have no choice, Pepe. Martinez told Papa we would all be killed if this partnership did not take place. From experience, you know he's telling the truth."

"What about Dan Keen?"

Juanita wouldn't meet Pepe's eyes. "What about him?"

"He's on our side, remember? He's the equalizer we needed, and he even carries the weight of U.S. deputy marshal. Martinez can't do anything with him around. Why else would he propose such a partnership? Especially now, after so many have been killed. It's his way of getting rid of Keen."

"Isn't that better than killing him? They missed him at the jail, but even Dan Keen's luck will run out. He isn't a match for Colin Wyatt—he's said that much himself."

Pepe scrutinized his sister. "You're worried about the lawman, aren't you?"

"I don't want anyone killed. There's been enough murder and bloodshed in El Hueco."

"Does Dan know about this marriage?"

"Father seemed to think that Martinez would tell him personally. Dan might be gone from the valley by this time."

"And you don't mind one bit, huh?" Pepe said.

"Why should I?" Juanita said a bit too quickly. "I care nothing for the bragging, arrogant gringo."

"You've never been able to lie to me, Juanita. Even as a child you couldn't keep secrets from me. I think you care more about Keen than you let on. Maybe you don't even know how you feel."

"Don't be ridiculous! Of course, I know how I feel."

"No matter," Pepe said shortly. "I won't let you marry Roberto Martinez!"

"What do you have to say about it? Father is the one who will give my hand in marriage."

But Pepe shook his head. "Do you hear yourself, Juanita? Can you sincerely mean what you're saying? Can you imagine yourself the wife of Roberto Martinez? How can you even consider such a thing?"

Juanita blushed, but her jaw remained firm, her eyes hard and resolute. "The fighting must stop. To refuse this wedding would only be an invitation to some more funerals. I won't be responsible for any more deaths."

"And I won't live in shame, Juanita," Pepe said tightly. "If I have to die, so be it.

But I won't let you make this sacrifice—I swear it!"

The banging on the hotel-room door brought Dan out of bed with a gun in his hand. Then he heard Juanita calling his name.

"Hold your horses!" he called back, pulling on his pants and boots. He took another moment to light the lamp before he opened the door.

The girl was out of breath. There was a pallor to her face and a redness to her eyes, as if she'd been crying.

Dan let her into the room, took a moment to peek down the hall, then closed the door. He didn't offer a greeting. Nor did he ask why she'd come. Juanita always had a reason for doing what she did. She would confide in him soon enough.

"You've heard about the wedding?" she asked.

"I've heard," he replied.

"I—I suppose Roberto Martinez came to see you personally."

"That's right. Spoke to me as if we were the best of friends. I didn't offer my congratulations."

"Are you leaving El Hueco?"

"The thought crossed my mind," Dan said.

She lowered her eyes. "You must think very poorly of me," she said softly. "I'm sorry if I've—if I've been cruel or unfair to you."

"Makes no difference now." He steadfastly kept all emotion out of his voice.

"My wedding will stop the killing. That's a worthwhile thing, don't you agree?"

"It is a bit out of your nature."

That brought the fire to her eyes. "You don't think very much of me, gringo, do you? You never have, and you never will."

"I don't think much of your latest idea, marrying Martinez. It's a dumb thing to do."

"Not if it saves the lives of my father and brother."

"Do you really think it would?" Dan asked.

"What do you mean?"

"I've studied men, Juanita. I know how to read most of them, and your betrothed stacks up with the worst of the lot. I wouldn't trust him to give me the right time of day."

"Well, I didn't come to get your opinion. I'm worried about Pepe. He swore he wouldn't let the marriage take place."

"Oh? And how does he plan to stop it?"

"I think he's going to try to kill Martinez. He left the house in a huff this evening and hasn't been seen since. He took his horse and his shotgun."

"And I suppose you want me to try and save the life of your husband-to-be."

"I couldn't care less about Martinez, but I don't want Pepe harmed."

"So you want me to drag out my horse in the middle of the night and ride toward a ranch somewhere out in the dark. Then if I don't get lost or shot in the night, I'm to find Pepe and talk some sense into him."

"You are wearing a badge now, remember?"

"I remember."

"Then it's your duty to stop a killing— whether it be Martinez or my brother."

"I've a mind to give up this job. No reason to get myself killed."

"But—but you . . ." she sputtered, finding herself flabbergasted at his nonchalance. "Dan Keen! You're a sworn officer of the law! You must save my brother's life!"

"I told you, I'm quitting. What happens here doesn't concern me any longer."

Her eyes filled up with bewilderment. "But...but he'll be killed. He has no chance against Roberto Martinez. Wyatt will be watching. They'll kill him for sure!"

"Then you won't feel you have to marry Martinez. That's what he has in mind, isn't it, sacrificing his life for yours?"

"You can't allow it!" Juanita snapped.

"If you can sacrifice yourself for Pepe, then he can sacrifice himself for you. I don't see why you expect me to interfere."

"You mean, you're just going to sit by, while my brother goes out and gets killed? What kind of man are you? What kind of blood does a gringo like you have in his veins? If I were a man, I'd—"

The door suddenly opened. Pepe was standing there, but he was not carrying a gun. In fact, he had no boots on. His eyes were full of sleep, and he wore no shirt.

"If you two are going to shout at each other, couldn't you do it somewhere else?"

"Pepe!" Juanita cried.

"We'll try and keep our voices down," Dan said. "Go back to bed."

Pepe closed the door and padded across

the hall to the room opposite Dan's. When his door shut, the fire really began to burn in Juanita's eyes.

"What a rotten, sneaking, filthy trick! You knew Pepe was safe all along! You made me think that you were leaving, that you didn't care what happened to Pepe or me!"

Dan stepped closer to Juanita. "So you really thought I'd walk out on you and your brother, huh?"

She backed up against the wall.

He kept coming closer. She tried to push him away, but he was having none of it. If this little minx was going to get him killed, the least she could do was give him one final kiss.

Again Juanita tried to push him away. But once his mouth found hers, once he pulled her to him, the fight was over. The pretense was gone. The haughty manner disappeared. Her arms slipped around Dan's neck, and she took his breath away with lips that were a mixture of sweet nectar and fire.

CHAPTER EIGHTEEN

Rico Lucinda had always wanted to feel like a big man. His mother used to slap him around, but that had come to a stop the day he'd hit back. The experience taught him women could be put in their place with a little physical force. He'd gotten carried away with his wife, beating her so badly that she died a few days later. If he ever went back to Texas, he would go to prison for that mistake.

Drinking usually made him get rough. All the girls in town knew about Rico and avoided being alone with him. But this young woman had come in by stage. She was tired of the long journey and would be stopping in El Hueco for the night. Rico took the opportunity to become acquainted with her. With all orders from Martinez telling Colin and the rest of them to sit tight, Rico had nothing better to do.

After plying her with plenty of drink, he

managed to take her out for a walk. They were moving toward the livery when he roughly grabbed her and started kissing her, if such harsh caresses could be called kisses.

Crying out, the woman tried to break away from Rico. That was when he began to hit her with the full force of his fists.

"All of you women are the same," he sneered. "You tease and toy with a man. Then you laugh in his face. No woman laughs in my face!"

The woman had a trickle of blood running from her lip, and one eye was swollen. She threw up her hands to ward off another barrage of blows.

Dan came in behind Rico, having decided to take a ride in the middle of the night. He'd planned to sneak into the Martinez house and arrest him—not that his plan had much chance of success.

Now his full attention was on the helpless woman and her attacker. Dan hurled Rico against the livery wall.

"You never learn, do you, Rico?" he said. "What will it take to make you stop acting like a wild animal?"

Rico gathered his senses about him, the

heavy drink giving him a greater recklessness than usual.

"No man pushes Rico Lucinda!" he snarled, his hand going for his gun. "I'm going to kill you, Keen!"

But he was too slow for the deputy marshal.

Dan only fired once, watching his adversary buckle at the knees. Rico would never harm another woman. His days of feeling like a big man were over. His gun was on the ground next to him. He died as he should, his face buried in the dust.

The woman hurried over to cling to Dan. She sobbed against his chest.

"He was crazy," she whimpered. "I...I was only—"

"What is going on here?" Juanita's voice cracked like a whip.

Dan turned to see the sleepy-eyed spitfire come toward him. There was no warmth in her face at seeing a woman in Dan's arms.

"Rico was getting rough again," he explained quickly. "I had to kill him."

Juanita hardly glanced at the man on the ground. She just took the woman forcibly away from Dan. Her eyes shone brightly. Her teeth were clenched with controlled anger.

"I'll see to this poor creature, Dan. If you want to comfort someone, you make darn sure that it's me!"

He grinned at her. "I didn't think you heard me leave the hotel."

"My brother is a wonderful person, but he snores loud enough to keep a bear from hibernating. Well, so you were sneaking out without saying good-by."

"I didn't want to worry you. I'd have been back first thing in the morning."

"Don't give me that!" she snapped. "If you expect me to love you, you'd better darn well let me know what you're up to. I don't intend to be taken for granted by some thoughtless gringo."

"Once we're married, I want to discuss the way you talk to me, Juanita. You don't show the proper respect."

"When I'm your wife, I might not want to be so proper and respectable. For now, you quit risking your life without warning me!"

"Sorry, Juanita. I didn't expect to run into Rico."

"Don't be sorry, just be healthy! I want you in one piece."

Several men had heard the shot and came over.

"A couple of you men see to Rico Lucinda. Tell Judge Haller that he tried to shoot me."

"Good riddance," one of the men grumbled.

"See there," another one said. "He was beating that poor gal that come in on the stage."

A third walked over and spat on the body, then faced Dan. "You done the entire human race a favor, Keen. Rico was lower than vermin."

Dan would have gone inside the barn for his horse, but the battered woman put out a hand, catching him by the sleeve.

"Thank you, mister," she said very softly.

"Like the man said, Rico was the scum of the earth." Dan sighed. "I only wish I'd have gotten here a little sooner."

"I'm taking care of the lady," Juanita said, pushing between them.

Dan put his hand under her chin and tipped her head back, kissing her very soundly. She allowed him that liberty, but her anger returned when the kiss was over.

"Don't you have any respect for me?

What will these people think, seeing you kiss me right out here in public?"

Dan chuckled. "They'll think that you're my woman, Juanita. They'll see that you've finally met your match."

"Get going!" she said briskly. "You said you'd be back by morning. Don't you be lying to me."

"The thought would never cross my mind, Juanita."

Two hours in the saddle put Dan into one of the hills above the Martinez spread. He had to wait for dawn to spot the outbuildings and check the lay of the ranch. Then he took up an unobtrusive vigil and bided his time.

Eventually riders were dispatched to move cattle or ride line. A little later the place was visited by a lone rider from the direction of El Hueco. He would bring news of Rico's death. The visitor didn't remain long, only speaking to Martinez in the front yard. When he left, there seemed to be no one but Martinez and one other man on the place. If there was a third person around, it was probably a cook or a maid— no one likely to make trouble.

Even as Dan made his way slowly toward the main house, the other man was sent riding off. That meant Martinez was probably alone. It couldn't have worked out better for Dan.

The front door wasn't locked, so the deputy marshal slipped into the house, hoping to surprise Martinez, who had begun to clean his guns.

"You figure on doing some shooting?" Dan asked.

"How dare you enter my house!" a shocked Martinez snapped. "What is the meaning of this intrusion?"

"Rico had a big mouth, Senor Martinez. Worse than that, he thought of himself as something of a gunman."

"What are you getting at?"

"I've got two witnesses to a confession." Dan grinned. "That confession will put a noose around your neck."

Martinez squinted at Dan. He couldn't tell whether the lawman was bluffing.

"I don't know what Rico might have said, but his word would not hold up in any court of law. Judge Haller would throw you out of his court for even mentioning that liar's name!"

"Perhaps," Dan said. "But I think Judge Larsen is more open-minded. I think he'll see that confession as the tool to put you behind bars until you're old and gray."

"You play a good hand of poker, Keen, but you've got nothing but air. I still hold the aces in this game."

"We'll just have to play all our cards out and see who has the high hand, Martinez. Let's go."

"You must be crazy!" Martinez was on his feet, but he was angry and defiant. "Colin will be along as soon as we leave here. He'll enjoy killing you! You are making the last mistake of your life!"

"I'll just have to worry about that later," Dan said. "Get your hat."

Martinez cursed. But he didn't try anything foolish. He knew he was no match for Dan Keen. All the same, he didn't like taking orders.

"I should have let my men kill you, Keen. I should have turned Wyatt loose on you when he asked my permission. You'll die hard, Keen. You ought to run and hide while you have the chance."

"Let's go, Martinez. You're scaring me to death with threats."

"It is no threat, Keen. Colin Wyatt will be right on your heels, and he'll kill you. As sure as the two of us are standing here together, he will shoot you down."

"You can cut the chatter, Martinez. I've got a pretty gal waiting for me in town. She'll be worried for my safety. Just remembering the way she kissed me last night, I can't keep from hurrying back to her."

That darkened the other man's face. It was obvious he knew who Dan was talking about.

"It will be too bad, Keen, but that little spitfire will die very shortly. I would have spared her for several months...until I grew tired of her. Now she will have to suffer and die with you."

"That would be preferable, Martinez," Dan replied roughly. "A death with me would have to be better than any life with you."

He pushed the land baron toward the door. And he tied Martinez's hands behind his back before they started for town.

CHAPTER NINETEEN

There was no jail now to hold Martinez in, but Dan found a solid smokehouse for his prisoner. He had no illusions about trying to take the man to Stockdale. Out in the open, Martinez's men would have found Dan an easy prey. The deputy marshal would have to wire for help or ask Larsen to come to El Hueco and oversee the trial himself.

He expected trouble before the first night, and he wasn't disappointed by Wyatt's crew. Bobby Leets was in town. Even watching the lawman take Martinez to the smokehouse, he was rubbing the spot on his head where Dan had clouted him. He disappeared into the saloon almost the same moment Dan spotted him. There was no question that Bobby would provide trouble.

Pepe was ready to help Dan. He had a

ten-gauge shotgun and a look of grim determination on his face. With such a
weapon in his hands, he would be a good
ally.

"I'm ready to guard your prisoner," Pepe
told Dan. "If necessary, I will kill him to
prevent his escape."

"Lock him up then, Pepe. Find a sheltered spot where you can watch the smokehouse. I'll be checking up on Bobby and
any others that are in town."

"I saw those two bounty hunters, Jeeter
and Gore. I think they're still around someplace."

"Thanks for keeping an eye out. Where's
your sister?"

"She returned to the ranch. I think she'll
try to get some of our men to come to town.
She had a feeling you would bring Roberto
Martinez in for trial."

"Smart kid, that sister of yours," Dan
said.

Pepe grinned. "Runs in the family."

"You are both dead men," Martinez
growled. "I will spit on your graves before
nightfall!"

Dan didn't offer any rebuttal. But he was
none too gentle as he helped Martinez—

whose hands were still tied—get off his horse.

"You are the big bull of the herd at the moment, Keen. You had better enjoy it!"

"Take Martinez away, Pepe."

Pepe stuck the barrel of his shotgun right under the prisoner's chin, and the pair marched off to the smokehouse.

Dan paid the two no more attention. He led his horse over to the hitching post in front of the saloon. He tied him off and loosened the gun in his holster. Then, with a deep breath to settle his nerves, he pushed the batwing doors aside and went into the saloon.

Bobby was at the bar. He had a bottle in front of him and was finishing a swig from his glass. Apparently, Bobby felt the need of some false courage.

Dan scanned the room, but he saw no sign of the two bounty hunters. He didn't like not knowing their whereabouts. Jeeter and Gore were as low as the dust and just as dirty. Stopping next to Bobby, Dan could see the uncertainty in the gunfighter's eyes.

"I'm giving you two seconds to get out of

town and never look back, Bobby Leets. If you refuse to go, I'll throw you in jail."

"What are you talkin' about? I ain't done nothing."

Dan's right fist exploded against Bobby's jaw. It knocked him to the floor.

"Time's up!" Dan said simply, standing over the dazed man. "You're under arrest."

Pulling the nearly unconscious man to his feet, Dan threw him over his shoulder and carried him out of the saloon. He squinted at the glare of the sun, then was knocked back a step by something slamming against his body.

Going down with Bobby still over his shoulder, Dan clawed his gun free. It was none too soon, for Jeeter Prize came out of the shadows with a smoking rifle in his hands. He lifted the gun to sight Dan in for another round.

Dan couldn't get free of the excess weight over his arm, but he shifted his gun around and fired. Then he rolled away from Bobby, bringing his weapon up for a better shot.

Jeeter seemed surprised that Dan could fire his gun, let alone move away from

Bobby with such agility. It caused him to hurry his next shot, the bullet whistling past Dan's cheek to slam into the wooden building at his back.

Thumbing his own gun, Dan put a sure round into the bounty hunter. At nearly the same instant, a loud boom resounded across the street. As Jeeter sank to his knees, Dan turned to see Pepe. He had the smoking shotgun in his hands. Not thirty feet from him, Gore Olson was sprawled on his back. From the size of the hole in his chest, there was little doubt that he was one back-shooter who would never kill again.

Pepe walked over and shoved Jeeter with the toe of his boot. The man didn't make any response. His eyes were wide open and staring at the sun.

"You got him square through the heart, Keen. Are you hurt?"

Dan dusted himself off and stood up. "I can't say just why, but I'm all right. Jeeter seemed to think he'd hit me right off. He was taking his time with that second shot."

"Lucky thing for you," Pepe said gravely. "By all rights, you should be the one lying on your back wondering if the Devil or Saint Peter was waiting to greet you."

"Here's the reason for that," the bartender said behind Dan. "Bobby took that there first bullet in the back. He's just as dead as the other two."

Dan shook his head. "Judge Larsen will have a fit. I wasn't supposed to let anyone else get killed!"

"Short of getting yourself killed, I don't see how it could have been avoided," Pepe said.

"Judge Larsen might have preferred that. I never have been one of his favorite deputy marshals."

"What now?" Pepe asked.

"Let's see to these three stiffs. The odds are no longer in Colin Wyatt's favor, so maybe he won't force another play."

"Do you really think so?"

Dan sighed, "No, but it sounded good when I said it."

The ranch house seemed much bigger to Colin Wyatt without Martinez stomping about. The cook had deserted, leaving without collecting the pay owed him. In fact, many of the crew had vanished upon hearing their boss had been taken into custody.

"What will you do?" someone asked.

Wyatt glanced up at Lorenzo Hoya. He hadn't even heard the man enter the house.

"You mean what will *we* do, don't you?" Wyatt said.

"No, Senor Wyatt. I know what I am going to do. I have my things packed and loaded on my horse."

"You're running?"

"It would seem to be the only way to remain healthy. Rico stayed, Bobby stayed, Jeeter and Gore stayed. I do not wish to stay behind in the same condition."

"I can take that fast-talkin' deputy marshal. We'll get the boss out of that smokehouse jail. Once Keen is dead, everything will be back to normal."

"It will not be so easy, Senor Wyatt. Several of the riders from the Mestas place have gone into town. Martinez is now guarded by several guns."

Colin removed his hat, running his hand through his hair. He sighed. Martinez had offered him what he was looking for, a place of his own, a ranch to ramrod. It would have been a great place to settle down. It still could be. There was only one thing in the way—Dan Keen!

"Will you go it alone, Senor Wyatt?"

"Tuck your tail and run, Lorenzo. I don't need you. I don't need anyone."

"That lawman is bad news for you, Senor Wyatt."

"Let me worry about my fate," Colin grated. "You get off the ranch pronto. Take the other cowards with you."

"None will go against the U.S. deputy marshal, Senor Wyatt. The gunmen are all dead now... all but you."

"I didn't ask for help!" Wyatt snapped. "Get the hell out of here—all of you yellow dogs!"

Lorenzo backed up to the doorway, his face flushed with anger. When he spoke, his voice was cold. "To most men in your position, I would say good luck. To you I say good riddance!"

Colin Wyatt's right-hand gun snapped up into his fist, but Lorenzo was gone.

With a new resolution filling his soul,

Colin decided to put an end to the man who'd ruined every plan he and Martinez had laid. It would be a real treat to watch Dan Keen go down under his guns.

CHAPTER TWENTY

"And if not for Pepe, you'd have been killed!" Juanita ranted on. "Are you in love with me or not?"

"Don't forget Bobby Leets," Dan reminded her, grinning at the woman's rancor.

"Oh, it's funny to you! But what about me? You've disgraced me by kissing me in public. If you don't marry me, I'll never be able to hold my head up again!"

"I'm a gringo—remember? I thought you'd just as soon I got myself shot."

"You could have offered me that choice before you kissed me right in front of the whole world!"

He chuckled, enjoying the exchange. He felt that Juanita was aware of what really lay ahead. Her fire and hot conversation helped keep the thought of Colin Wyatt from Dan's mind. If death was coming to him at El Hueco, he could at least forestall thinking about it.

"Speaking of kissing, why don't you come a little closer. I could use some comfort about now."

Juanita waved one finger back and forth as if he'd just asked for something naughty. "Not until we are married, gringo. You've humiliated me in public for the last time."

Dan looked around, knowing that only the two of them were in the hotel room. "Who's to see?"

"Being seen doing something isn't all important. I would know that you were taking advantage of me. Once we are married, you can kiss me all you like."

"Seems that you ought to entice me a little, Juanita. I might forget just how sweet your lips are and back out of this shotgun wedding."

The girl's eyes were aglow, sparkling like clear spring water. The slightest trace of a mischievous smile was on her soft lips. She came slowly forward, as if to heighten his impatience.

"If you promise...only one, gringo. You shall not take liberties with me."

"The thought would never occur to me,"

Dan said with all the innocence he could muster.

Even as the young spitfire came into his arms, Dan could hear the approach of footsteps in the hall. Since Juanita didn't pull away, he drew her still closer. He was just warming to the thrill of her fiery lips when Pepe opened the door.

For a younger brother, Pepe had better than average manners. He was good enough to remain silent and stand behind the door, awaiting the break between Dan and Juanita.

"What's up, Pepe?" Dan asked, a bit out of breath.

"Colin Wyatt is coming into town. Fernandez was up the trail keeping watch. He says the man is coming in alone."

"That's something of a break for us."

"It only takes one bullet to kill you," Juanita said tightly. "Don't give that murderer a chance. Kill him from ambush!"

"What a cold-blooded vixen you are," Dan remarked, shaking his head.

Juanita's eyes filled with tears. "No one would fault you, Dan. No man can face up to Colin Wyatt's speed. I don't want you in a coffin."

"I don't intend to end up in a coffin if I can help it. But the law is the law. I'll have to arrest him."

"You want me to back you up?" Pepe asked.

"Not this time. You set up some kind of defense over at the smoke shack. If I fail, you'll have to kill Wyatt any way you can."

"I'll have Bernardo stand by with a rifle. If I see Wyatt coming, I'll blow him right out of existence with my ten-gauge."

"Get going then."

Juanita caught hold of Dan's arm, preventing him from following Pepe. She encircled his waist with her arms, standing very close.

"If you don't come back to me, Dan, I'll forever hate all gringo men. You wouldn't want that, would you?"

"Guess not. And when the likes of Wyatt and Martinez are behind bars or swinging at the end of a rope, I'm turning in my badge. You can tell your father that I'm not such a bad hand with cattle."

"You come back and we'll tell him together."

Dan tipped the young woman's head back, kissing her ever so gently. Then he

was striding from the room with a rifle. He
had a man to meet, a man who'd killed
many in gunfights, a man with the odds on
his side.

Colin stopped his horse at the edge of
town, watchful for some kind of ambush.
He didn't expect it from someone like
Keen, but then the lawman had to know he
was no match for Wyatt's guns.

Dan pulled his Henry repeater rifle from
the scabbard next to his saddle. He was
maybe a hundred yards from the gunman,
but the shadows hid him. He could see the
man thinking. Even as Colin got down
from his horse, Dan knew the man's mind
was working. He wouldn't take a chance on
his horse jumping or shying away. Colin
Wyatt was a professional, a man who could
kill with great care.

Rather than make the gunman look for
him, Dan walked out into the street. He
cocked the rifle, jacking in a live round.
Then he stood steadfast in the middle of
the street.

"You're under arrest, Wyatt!" he called,
his heart pounding so hard he could barely
hear his own words. "Throw down your

guns and raise your hands!"

As expected, Colin didn't surrender on the spot. Instead, the man started toward Dan. His hands went down to the guns he was wearing on each hip. He strode forward like a man possessed, eyes ablaze, his total concentration on Dan Keen.

Dan lifted his rifle, aligning the sights. Colin didn't seem to notice, coming closer with each step.

"Stop where you are!" Dan called.

But Wyatt kept coming.

"Stop! Or I'll kill you!" Dan warned.

Wyatt was almost within pistol range. Dan planned to shoot him before his pistols could become useful.

"Don't try it, Wyatt! I'll have to..."

Colin kept walking. At the last moment Dan found that something inside him was forcing him to wait till the gunman had a chance too.

The two got ready to shoot at the same instant—then something made Colin trip, deflecting the bullets from his two guns. But Dan's shot went right home.

Without ejecting the spent cartridge, the lawman started toward the gunman, who was slowly falling to the ground.

"I would have got you, Keen. I almost had you. You're just too damn lucky." Those were his last words.

Dan pulled the star from his chest and dropped it onto the lifeless body. He never wanted to kill again. He would bring Martinez to justice. But no more shooting.

Even as Dan walked away from the body of Colin Wyatt, Juanita was running to him. At last the war was over...life was just beginning again.